Christine Balint's first novel, *The Salt Letters*, was shortlisted for The Australian/Vogel's Literary Award and published by Allen & Unwin in 1999. Her second novel, *Ophelia's Fan*, was released in 2004. Christine's work has been published to critical acclaim in Australia, The United States, Germany and Italy. She is currently developing a body of work set in eighteenth-century Venice.

Christine has a PhD in Creative Arts from The University of Melbourne and taught for seven years in RMIT's Graduate Writing Program. She teaches in the Creative Writing Program at The University of Melbourne.

*For Imogen and Raphael*

This project was made possible by the
Foundation of Australian Literary Studies
regional writers sponsorship

9781922267610 (print) | 9781922598363 (digital)


Brio Books
Level 8, 67 Castlereagh Street, Sydney NSW 2000, Australia
www.briobooks.com.au

Internal design and typesetting © Brio Books 2020
Cover illustration and design by Sam Paine,
www.sampaine.com
Edited by Alice Grundy

# CHRISTINE BALINT

*b*

BRIO

# 1

When you are not raised a *gentildonna*, you spend time with your brother and the neighbourhood boys kicking an inflated pig's bladder in the laneway. It bounces against archways, flying in unpredictable directions. Sometimes, you kick it so far and fast that one of the boys has to dive into the lagoon to retrieve it. In the summer, the boys have bare feet. By the time they turn six, their feet are hardened like rosin.

I was reared on water and fish like a bird. So much fish that I know its smell is in the pores of my skin. When I walk in the market, I notice a lady's maid screwing up her nose and stepping away from me. In the night I lie awake, wondering if the stench will ever leave my skin.

As I prepare to leave, I spend a lot of time at my toilette. To mask my scent, I gather rosemary from the windowsill and rub the leaves into my skin. I take the smoke-scented nightdress, underclothes and dress hanging before the fire and fold them into my trunk. I nestle my violin case into the fabric.

Along with the other items in my trunk, there is a heavy linen bedspread that Mamma worked on for three years. Although she can no longer smell it, she knows about the odour of fish that permeates our room; she washed the bedspread in lemon soap bought from a merchant at the Rialto. It dried stiff in the sirocco wind over the lagoon last summer, the smell of salt lingering in its thread. I know what it cost her in meat and fruit to attain those embroidery silks. How many years of reading she lost for the sake of those tiny yellow calendula on the crisp white linen. All so that I have something of hers to keep me warm at night.

My trunk also contains a small painting to put upon the wall of my new room, a sketch of a *barca* completed by my brother Lionello for my sixteenth birthday last spring. Lionello was not born with the hands — or the stomach — of a fisherman. Although he has a large build, his fingers are fine and suited to delicate work. While Lionello would have preferred to join the artists' guild, Papà could not introduce him there. Instead, the priest, Padre Porto, found Lionello a harpsichord tuner with whom to serve out an apprenticeship. While Papà scours the ocean with his net, Lionello — in his rare idle moments — sketches his father's craft.

On the final afternoon at home, I greet Papà returning from the lagoon with his fishing bucket. As his sodden boots leave puddles on the worn timber floor, he leans in to kiss me with his sweaty sheen and the pungent, familiar smell of fish.

Although he holds the bucket still, something is moving inside, rivulets flowing down its timber sides.

'What is it, Papà?'

'Pietro! Your boots!' Mamma says.

'Not my boots. Lucietta's boots. I will make them shine!'

He takes the lid from his bucket, and I peer inside. The creature is still alive, staring with its black eyes, its tiger-striped pillow body floating in the shallow water, its tentacles curling aimlessly.

'How?' I ask.

'Ink. We will make polish.'

Mamma busies herself with the copper pot while Pietro slices the squid, pouring its ink into a clay basin, leaving its slimy innards on a tray.

'We could fry it for supper, Silvia. What do you think?'

'I want nothing to do with it.'

And so, Pietro takes the remains out to the *calle* and drops them on a stone near the back door, where the neighbourhood cats soon devour them. For weeks afterwards, the neighbours will remark upon the sudden darkening of the cats' whiskers and will step nervously away from Pietro and his large, blackened hands. But I will be long gone by then.

Lionello works all morning blending cooking fat and squid ink in Mamma's iron pot for my boots. He buffs them in the afternoon with an old dishrag, and you have to look very closely to see that still they are scuffed and worn at the toes. Sitting at the kitchen table, Lionello spits on my boots to draw out the lustre.

In the evening, Mamma helps me wash my hair in a clay basin by the kitchen fire. You would not know it dried in the smoke, for it is soft, shining and golden, pinned up like that of a *gentildonna*. Mamma says I must stand straight and show them who I am right from the first moment. Never look down, she says. Never let anyone think she is superior to you.

Mamma does not come with me to the Derelitti. I ask her not to, and this time she listens. She hands me a small cake wrapped in linen, embracing me for a moment. I breathe in her smell of salted cooking fat. She drops her arms to her sides, and I step back.

'May God love and protect you. Go with her, Lionello. Keep her safe.'

She wipes under her eyes and covers her face with her hands. Lionello stares at his feet. Then he bends and picks up my box as though it contains feathers. I follow him out the door, my vision blurred — and the breath gone from my lungs — a heavy ache in my heart.

'Lionello, I can manage,' I whisper in the *calle* some moments later, returning to myself. I suppose he thinks I cannot. I sigh; I walk tall with my arms free. Delivery boys and washerwomen pass by with their arms full.

I walk unencumbered over the Rio dei Mendicanti. The marble facade of the Mendicanti orphanage glistens in the sunlight, the light reflecting from the canal. On the far side of the orphanage, the red brick Basilica dei Santi Giovanni e Paolo is in shade. My cloak billows with a gust of wind. Mamma used the last of her red thread to cover up the moth holes by pale candlelight. If you examine my cloak in sunlight, it will reveal tiny scars. Lionello thumps behind me, breathing heavily now. He re-soled my boots and raised the heels slightly with some off-cuts from the luthier. I sway on the pitted cobblestones. A nun is leading a neat line of uniformed girls towards the canal. A man whistles to his large brown dog, which squats on the pavement. A crowd of pigeons stands in the *calle*. They shiver and fluff up their feathers until they are soft grey balls huddling on the stones.

I have been inside the church of the Derelitti many times. I found my place among the crowds: from the dukes and barons to the flower seller coming inside to escape the bitter wind whipping off the lagoon. In quiet moments, I tipped back my head to examine the fresco: angels offering protection for the church and its people, their gowns wafting in a cloudy sky. Listening to the angelic cadences wafting from above, I imagined standing in the choir loft: the dark and cramped balcony from where the girls made their music. I wondered about the enclosed life in a crowded building. Afterwards, I returned to the cold, damp apartment with its fish scales in the basin and its smoky cooking fire. If I stayed with Mamma, there would be no other future for me. One day, I would have my own fisherman for a husband, my own dingy smoke-filled room, my own fish heads to feed to the neighbourhood cats.

Mamma had requested of the Pietà that I be allowed to stay with her until the age of sixteen to learn how to live in a family. From when I was very young, she said I would have to leave to find a better life: a husband who would appreciate my gift for music and keep me in rooms that were warm and light with windows that opened out over the Canale

Grande. I did not question this. But there is still a small girl inside me who just wants to kick a ball and run in the laneway with Lionello and the boys.

I slow as my new home comes into relief. The building is pure white stone with strong men draped in cloth holding up its columns. It is an orphanage, a hospital, a refuge, a music school, a church. Filled with the vulnerable, it requires the backbones of men — it seems — to hold their weight.

'Lionello . . .'

He stops as though waiting for me to speak. I both want and do not want him gone. The door is heavy, and it creaks as I open it. Lionello's arms are full of my past: faded clothing, crisp linen, fraying pages and a violin — it is not much to show for a life. A woman sits at a desk near the door. She wears white robes. She looks up from a piece of parchment covered with dark, hurried musical notes.

I open my mouth, but the words do not come. A slight hum emerges on my breath. Then I hear myself say, 'I am Lucietta . . . the new violinist.'

'They are expecting you; I will find the *priora*.'

A wrought-iron grille runs the entire length of the room. It begins to the left of the entranceway and travels to the back left corner: a transparent wall. There are wooden chairs on either side of the grate. Beyond the grille are the white stone walls and another door leading inside building.

The woman stands; she is tall. She walks to the back corner of the grille and opens a door there, locking herself in with an iron key from around her neck. From my place in the foyer, I see her shadow disappearing into the building.

Lionello stands behind me, still clutching my box.

'You can put it down now, Lionello.'

He places it on the tiles and turns to me. I pause for a moment between two lives: the one outside and the one inside. I lean in and kiss his rough cheek, this morning's cheese still on his breath.

'Goodbye. Bring Mamma and Papà to see me soon!'

He sniffs. 'Bye,' he mutters. He lumbers back to the door, his feet heavy. Then, he is gone.

Once inside the locked wrought-iron door, I will not be free to leave. For a moment, I imagine catching up to Lionello. We could walk home together. Life would continue as before. But I yearn not for the most recent past. I dream of earlier, simpler times.

The windows behind me let in a small amount of light. Footsteps grow louder, and an older woman emerges from the corridor with the woman from the desk. She is also robed in white.

'I am the *priora*.'

I shake her hand, which is firm and cold and damp as a fish. Her face is alabaster and grained as marble. 'Bring your things this way. Let me show you to your room.'

I look back down at the trunk and wonder if I will be able to lift it. All these years protecting my hands and my arms from heavy work, and now — when I am finally to work as a musician — I have to lift my life's sum of possessions. I bend and clasp my arms around the trunk, surprised at its heaviness.

We step through the side door at the back of the grille, and the *priora* turns the iron key: we are locked in. I shudder.

I follow the *priora* into a passageway; winter sunlight glints off hardened grey streaks, the bird droppings like dry paint. We pass a door to the church on the left, and a faint smell of sweet incense fills the air. A cool draught wafts through the building. The light coming through the high windows forms little squares on the opposing walls. My boots beat loudly on the tiles; the *priora* walks silently in her slippered feet. I cannot lighten my tread with the weight I carry. I try to steady and soften my breathing.

We pass a large hall on the right where a nun is setting long tables. We climb a long spiral staircase, wide and free-standing. It hangs in the air like a mast. The *priora* does not speak as she leads me through the building, nodding to a woman sweeping the stairs as we pass.

'I hope you will be comfortable here,' she says,

pausing before a heavy oak door at the top of the stairs. She pushes it open. I am breathless, my heart-beat pulsing in my ears.

The room is cavernous with vaulted ceilings, echoing with girls' voices. Some are sitting on white quilts pulling on their woollen stockings.

'Quiet!' The woman's voice is shrill. The girls pause as though she has cast a spell and made them statues. For a moment, there is silence.

'This is Lucietta. She is our new violinist. Please help her find everything she needs.'

Each girl turns to stare at me. Some of them exchange glances. Gradually, they look away. I find myself staring at my boots; their lucid sheen seems ridiculous now.

The *priora* leads me through the room to my bed. 'Here you are.' She tightens her lips into a kind of smile. The bedhead is faded, the pillow a perfect dome beneath a white bedspread. For a moment, I long for my polished bed from home. I place the trunk on the floor.

'You will need to change.' She nods at a shapeless white garment upon the bed. 'The white symbolises purity.' Her voice fades like an echo. For a moment, she is absent from herself. Then, she meets my eye once more, pointing to the drawers beside the bed.

'These are for your belongings. You must use the regulation bedding and clothing. Maestra Francesca will be here shortly to talk about your work.'

I try to ask about Mamma's bedspread, but she is already walking away. As she passes each girl, she points at creases in their bedding, handkerchiefs on the floor. I push the robes aside and sit. The mattress is hard. I am in the middle of an ocean of beds stretching in every direction. The walls have the foggy uncertainty of clouds.

I open my wooden box, its exterior sawn, sanded and lacquered by Lionello. On top is my battered violin case. Inside, my violin is shiny and mottled; it smells faintly of woodsmoke and frying fish. I breathe in the air from home and tried to quell the tears. For a moment, I clasp the violin to me. I place it back in its case and reach inside the trunk to unpack the undergarments, plain white nightgown and violin music. Crouching beside the timber drawers, I tug at the one on top. It sticks, and the drawers rock unsteadily. The wood is faded and scratched. I wonder about all the girls before me who similarly unpacked their lives into it. Where are they now?

I stand and smooth my navy day dress, looking down at the white uniform, so like a nun's habit, that I will wear from now on. I look around. The other girls have returned to their tasks. There is nowhere private, it seems. Bowing my head, I begin unbuttoning my dress. I let it fall to the marble floor and step out of it, the petticoat floating and thread-bare, the once white fabric now closer to grey, a grey that would let the light through and illuminate my figure in brighter light. Now, I reach and pull the rough woollen garment over my head. Immediately, I am weighed down, and I see why the others move so slowly and steadily. I reach down to untie and remove my boots, pulling the slippers over my toes. Although no one has measured my feet, the slippers are a good fit, soft and comfortable, their dark leather sealing in the warmth.

I unpack Lionello's sketch. Fine, strong hands crafted the boat illustrated here: my father's hands and yet not my father's hands. The *barca* sails upon a choppy sea. I am on board with Papà and Mamma in the drawing, my hair flying in the wind. I feel behind my head for the intricate knot Mamma tied there.

I reach into the box to remove the bed linen. As I lift it, a golden thread catches on the side of the box. I pull, and the thread snaps. The linen is surprisingly weighty, and I place it — still neatly folded — upon the bed. The snagged thread has warped one of the flowers. As I pull at the fabric in dismay, the golden calendula begins to unravel.

———

Ever since the founders first built stumps into the

mud to raise dwellings out of the lagoon, all of Mamma's ancestors fished for a living. When she first met Pietro at the fish market, Mamma knew her family would allow her to go to him, and they could build a life on fish — just as her parents had. She worked as a kitchenhand and looked forward to an independent life in her little room. She wanted to be allowed to eat the meals she prepared and not merely the off-cuts.

Following her marriage, Mamma became pious. She came to believe it was not right that a man should be paid for pilfering God's creatures from the sea. After all, the fish are not of man's making; how can they be seen as his? She said a man has ownership of fish in the same way a thief has ownership of the sack of coins he found in the Bank of the Republic or a moneylender's hands. Mamma also knew that, at any moment, God could take the fish away or send a sickness through the lagoon or a high tide that would fill the water with rubbish from the streets: vegetable peelings, chicken bones, soapy water and paint — things that could make fish and people sick. So Mamma set out to ensure she could also earn a living and, like other Venetian artisans, that was through selling what she made.

After Mamma birthed Lionello, she discovered that her body could make as much milk as a nanny goat. Her own mother sewed her a scarf to wear around her shoulders and cover up the large milky stains on her dress. She was ashamed in those early, exhausting days of motherhood — and had not enough dresses or underwear to make sure she was always clean and dry. The very saltiness of the lagoon seemed to be seeping out of her body. She could barely keep up with washing cloths and swaddling for the child without having to wash one of her two dresses every day. And during the damp winter, nothing would dry. She hung a small wooden rack before the fire, but it could take a week for a woman's dress to dry there in the smoke.

Soon there came word from the Pietà Foundling Home, near San Marco, that one of the wet nurses had finished and retired: her milk had turned thin and sour and then, finally, had disappeared. New small mouths called out in hunger. The night after Padre Porto told Mamma this she did not sleep, the soul-numbing screams drifting to her in the wind. The next morning after Pietro went out in his boat, she swaddled Lionello and put him in a carry basket. She covered her shoulders and marched on foot to the Pietà. Even as she approached the walls, she could hear the cries of hunger and the nuns' anxious raised voices. For all their learning and all the nourishment of their souls, these virgins had nothing to sustain a tiny life.

Mamma was taken straight to the *priora*. She

placed the basket holding a sleeping Lionello at her feet. Within two minutes, I was in her arms, limp and tiny, eyes only half-open, nuzzling her chest, opening my mouth. I had just been retrieved from the revolving stone cradle in the courtyard, the *scaffetta*, and I yawned for my breakfast.

Later, after she took me home and fed me, Mamma unwrapped the swaddling to inspect me. It was not unusual for a foundling to be missing a limb or a finger. When she lifted me into the air and saw that I was fully formed, an unevenly cut rectangle of parchment fluttered to the floor. My birth mother had left me with half a carefully painted wind chart showing the direction of the sirocco wind blowing hot and dry from the Sahara Desert. The wind brought rain and storms; in the south, it could bring blood rain. In Venice at high tide, the sirocco wind would bring *acqua alta* and a feeling of unease. For herself, my real mother had kept the *ponente*, the wind blowing from the west — the direction of the sunset. She had also kept the *tramontane* — the north wind — and anything foreign or uncanny. If she ever came for me, I would know her by the perfect reunification of the wind chart, the two halves slotting together with a barely discernible seam as though they had never been separated.

Mamma's first mistress had taught her to read. Mamma was poor, but the priest helped keep her in books. Each leatherbound volume would be with her for just a few days. She pored over them by lamplight, committing passages to memory so they would remain with her. She said *The Iliad* was too preoccupied with battle. She preferred the journey beyond the known world in *The Divine Comedy*. It was a woman, Beatrice, who led Dante to heaven. Mamma used to say: never let it be said that I sucked the milk of a woman with a feeble mind.

Mamma's milk became her bread. Baskets of fruit and cheese would arrive and more baskets containing babies not a week old, to be fed. She could manage three at a time while keeping house for Pietro. Later, she remembered each child by the way it sucked, how it clenched its fist or clutched gently at her breast. Whether it gulped heartily at the milk or sucked softly in its sleep. Not one died. Mamma was proud of this. Once the infants grew big enough to take the fruit and cheese, Pietro took them back. Mamma would wipe her eyes, knowing the rosy-cheeked child with grasping arms would soon forget her. She asked permission to raise just one girl: I was the one she kept.

As a wet nurse, Mamma said she was dependent on no one: she sold fluid of her own making. Papà made his living by selling dead things stolen from the sea. Mamma made her living by selling the stuff of life created by her own body. In the words of

Mamma: I was her first customer, and I stayed.

Later, I would wonder whether my birth mother had been a noblewoman or a woman from the lower classes. Perhaps life had prevented an acceptable union between my birth parents, so I had been cast out.

My real father had left instructions and funds to secure my musical education. It seemed likely he was from one of the noble families, which were all listed in the Golden Book. In my dreams, I studied the book until I found him. In reality, he was a feature-less man I might never meet.

After I turned seven, Mamma took me to my lessons at the church with Padre Porto twice a week. In addition to my father's endowment, she paid him in biscotti or fried fish wrapped in paper.

Mamma would stand behind the door, listening to me recite the catechism in Latin.

'You sounded just like the priest!' she would whisper to me on the way home, pushing a small piece of biscotto into my hand.

As I grew older, Padre Porto lent me poetry to read and trained me to write with a neat hand. When I stood to recite Petrarch's 'On the Solitary Life', which I had memorised in Latin, he shook his hand at my accent.

'No! Not Veneziano like a fishwife! Latin like a Cleric! Again from the top!'

Padre Porto and the music school made the

arrangements for my violin lessons at Santa Maria dei Derelitti. My teacher, Don Domenico, learned to look past my threadbare dresses and scuffed shoes. He taught me how to read music at great speed and write perfectly even semiquavers without blotting my pen so that they looked as though a printing machine had made them. If he could not find enough bowing exercises for me, he wrote more.

Because my fingers were my future, Mamma was always careful of them. She did not let me cook or clean: the onions, saltwater and soap would make the skin as dry and cracked as hers. Mamma told me I was meant for better things and that, one day, she would have to let me go.

Our apartment was just one room containing a hearth and table and three wooden beds. The timber came from a shipwreck that Papà had discovered in his early days of fishing. He had saved seven floundering passengers who had been on their way to Murano for a picnic when two boats collided. One of the boats quickly began to list and fill with water. Papà rescued the passengers in his small boat and took them to the mainland. The owner of the sunken vessel, Vendramin, offered Papà the salvaged timber in gratitude. Papà hammered it together with nails purchased from the Arsenale. He sanded, oiled and polished the wood. For the first sixteen years of my life, I spent every night upon the remains of a wrecked boat, this life raft leading to my dreams. The distant sound of lapping water softened Lionello's snoring, Mamma's sighs and Papà's snores.

I do not remember a time prior to learning the violin. The instrument always felt like another limb, another voice. It was not separate from my body. I always practised my violin at sunrise. Papà would get up while it was still dark and leave the house with his nets. The sound of the front door closing would wake me. Mamma would already be stoking the fire, using the large black pot to boil water she had collected from the rainwater cistern the previous day — so we could clean our faces without freezing. I would rise in my nightclothes, cover myself with a woollen cloak and stand by the tiny, smeared window looking out onto the *calle*. From there, I would make out the grey shapes of women at the well. I would see pigeons jostling for crumbs shaken out into the square. I would take up my violin and play the morning song. I often practised with my eyes closed to intensify my attention on the sound and block out the smoke. Lionello ate his bread each morning to the rhythm of my playing.

I was something of a curiosity in the *calle*. The girl who did not sully her hands but instead used them to make music from a wooden box. At times, I drew weary looks from the neighbouring families.

We heard their clattering pots, their doors slamming and their shouting. My toccatas and fugues pushed their way inside neighbouring houses like sunlight. Sometimes, I was invited to perform at birthday celebrations or anniversaries. Mamma would wear her cleanest house dress, leaving her apron behind. She would perch in the background on a small wooden stool, grinning openly while the revellers danced and clapped and sang. One evening, I played at the seventh birthday celebration of a neighbour's child. Anna was a playfellow of mine, just two years younger. The skin on her hands was red raw from helping her mother in the laundry. The soles of her feet were hardened from running on the cobblestones barefoot.

'Lucietta's going to be a musician, is she?' Anna's mother asked as we were leaving, rocking a toddler in her arms.

'Yes,' my mother replied.

'How can you be certain?'

'It is not in my hands.'

'They don't take just anyone, you know. What if she is not good enough? What will she do then? Teach her some useful things, Silvia. Don't let her get too soft.'

Mamma had taken me in and followed all directives from the Pietà concerning my education and musical training. She believed that if she followed these instructions, my musical and marital future were assured. She did not tell me precisely whose decisions she followed. In this way, I did not know my own story. The story I knew well — that of life with Mamma, Papà and Lionello — was a borrowed history. I clung to it.

Within the family of Mamma and Papà and Lionello, I was the first person to be educated. I was the first person who could read music like a story. I was the first person who could sing a song that was written on the page.

At sixteen, I submitted my beautifully handwritten application to live and work and complete my musical training at the Derelitti. It contained my baptism certificate and a reference from Padre Porto, which presented my unblemished church attendance record over the previous three years. I was unable to present a certificate of legitimacy without my parents' names. However, I submitted a recommendation from Don Domenico. Upon the basis of these documents, I was admitted for an audition.

## 2

I am sitting on my firm bed, watching the dust floating in the light from the windows, a beam of sunshine creating a shaft so solid I feel as though I could climb it.

'Lucietta?' I startle and focus on the girl standing in front of me. Her right arm is at her side; her left arm is a loose sleeve.

'My name is Regina.'

I try to smile, but there is a tightness to my lips. I wonder if I am grimacing.

'We are not supposed to talk — but if you whisper, they think it's prayers . . . You must wash. It's the first thing we have to do when we arrive. Let me show you the bathroom.'

I stand, and we walk together. Other girls turn to stare at us as we go. They do not try to hide it.

'We have a little time now until "none", the office after rest. Do you know the daily offices?' She speaks fast and sotto voce so that it is hard to make out her words. I look at her lips, and they are not moving. It takes me a moment of silence to understand.

'A little. From church. And lessons.'

'You will need to know it all by heart. All the words and music must be within you.'

We continue down the spiral staircase. When a nun passes by on her way up the stairs, Regina looks piously down at her feet. I do the same. The nun stares at me. Her footsteps fade and once we can no longer hear them, Regina mutters, 'Suora Barbara. She's friendly once she gets to know you. But she's never lived outside and is mistrustful.'

We walk through the refectory where a maid is wiping one of the long tables. Behind the serving area, the staircase leads to the basement. We descend into darkness — a place in shadows where the air is chilled by stone. At the bottom of the stairs, I can smell the smoke of a kitchen fire to the right. There are women's voices loud and brash, pots clanging. Regina nods to the left; I follow her to a large room with high laundry piles. A large-bosomed woman in a white apron is clutching a habit in her arms.

'Regina, my dear, who is this?'

'This is the new violinist, Lucietta.'

The woman walks closer. I step back as she stares intently at me.

'Do you still have your hair?'

I nod in confusion, looking at Regina.

'We have to cut it off. Vanity — and lice.'

I stare at Regina, shocked at this betrayal. She has brought me here as though to a guillotine. Regina looks down at the pink fingernails of her only hand. Part of her is missing, absent, never to be returned. 'Don't worry,' Regina says softly, 'we can still make it beautiful.'

I swallow a sob.

'I will bring her back,' the woman says.

Regina puts her hand on my arm. 'It won't hurt,' she says. 'Will it, Vittoria?'

'I've never hurt a mouse,' she says. 'Sit down, dear,' Vittoria pushes my shoulders down to seat me on a dull timber chair. I shudder and close my eyes. I hear Regina make her way slowly up the steps.

As Vittoria tugs the pins free, she plucks individual hairs from my scalp. She unthreads the strip of silk, leaving me unadorned and bare. She hands it to me, and I place it in my pocket. I am ashamed of my nakedness.

The scissors are cold against my neck as she hacks at my hair. She tugs at it; I can feel she is leaving the edges jagged and uneven. Tears begin to drop from my closed eyelids. And then I see Mamma with her rosy cheeks, yesterday — was it only yesterday — washing my hair in sweet-smelling soap, running the comb through as it dried by the fire. The firelight made it shine and glow. She tied it up then with the silk ribbon and pins. If I had a silk gown, I could have passed for a noblewoman crossing the Rialto. And now, all that work has been undone; I am as unworthy as my origins.

Vittoria does not offer me a glass of any kind to observe her work. She is perplexed when I stand and stumble from the chair. 'Now, dear, you know you must wash the streets from your skin?' When I do not reply, she continues, 'One of the baths in there still has water in it, though I'm not sure how warm it is . . .'

At home, whenever we spoke of my new life at the Derelitti, I heard the words 'music' and 'future'. I would find myself among other educated girls. I would be at home. But instead, I am being stripped of all I have ever known.

The bathroom is all dark corners and large polished basins. One basin at the back is half-filled, though I cannot discern the contents in the near darkness. I reach in the basin and feel grains of sand or salt between my fingers. There is a rough bar of soap and a coarse drying sheet. I use one corner of the drying sheet and dip it in the water, telling myself that the particles will float to the bottom. That I am cleaning myself to begin anew.

I blot my skin with the drying sheet. After washing, my body smells like the silt of the lagoon. I pull my robes on, fitting the wimple tightly over the rough ends of my hair. I stand tall, push my shoulders back. I will blend in now. I will be the same as every other girl in a white habit smelling of silt, roughly chopped hair invisible beneath the wimple.

On my way up the stairs to the refectory, I hear voices singing. The sound is distant at first, echoing in a vaulted ceiling. From the refectory, I walk along the corridor towards the front of the building. The sound is coming from the church to the right. I stop before the side door into the church; I dare not open it.

Behind me, the main building is still and silent as though everyone has left. I hear a sweet polyphonic sound from behind the door, the voices weaving, floating. And then they stop, the echo snuffed out like a candle. I hear the rising tenor, the priest's powerful voice, '*In Nomine Patris et Filii, et Spirutus Sancti* . . .' I slide softly to the floor and lean my back against the wall, eyes closed, head in my hands. The mass washes over me like a salve.

After some time, I hear bodies moving. There are muttering voices. I stand and hurry back through the corridor, up the stairs to the dormitory. The room is empty and silent; I do not know what I am supposed to be doing. I consider curling up beneath my blankets. Would anyone notice my absence?

I am staring into the growing darkness when Regina appears in the doorway. 'I was looking for you! Come now, we have rehearsal. Bring your violin.'

She leads me to a smaller door at the back of the dormitory. 'Just so you know, you can sign in to use the practice room between four and six every day. Before vespers. But when the whole coro is rehearsing, we use the church.' We step through the door into a dark passage. I pause. She smiles. 'In case you're ever running late for matins, this corridor delivers you straight to the choir loft.'

We emerge into the church balcony through a door below the organ. Above the pipes, the instrument is bordered in gilded vines and cherubs. The organist sits slightly elevated, a side mirror enabling her to see the conductor who will be behind her. A group of seven girls is standing with heads bowed, whispering. Nearer to the grille, a girl is tuning a viola. There are eight string players in all. I look around and spot four violins, two violas and two violoncelli. A woman a little older than me stands before the grille. She holds a violin bow, the violin tucked under her arm, muttering to the child in front of her.

'That's Maestra Francesca. And the little girl is Tonina.'

As I lift my violin to tune it, I watch Regina walk to join the group of girls at the back. The other girls smile at her. They pat her shoulder. They speak sotto voce. I move closer to where Maestra Francesca is standing. She looks up as girls mutter and arrange pages on music stands. She meets my eye. 'You must be Lucietta.' There is a quick impatience in her hands; she puts down her violin and bow to gather up a thick wad of parchment and a small leather-bound book. 'Welcome to the Derelitti. You come highly recommended by Padre Porto and Don Domenico. You have a generous patron.'

I am unbalanced for a moment. What does she know of my father? She hands me the pages. 'This is the music for the ordinary mass. And here is the book of liturgy.'

The paper is thick, yellow, furred at the edges. The notes are scrawled, thin and hurried. The leather binding of the small book is soft and pliable. Maestra Francesca points at a place in front of her. I sit between Tonina, swinging her legs, and a girl similar to me in age, gripping a violoncello with her knees. The wimple over the child's hair is crooked, leaving the lopsided ends of her hair exposed. She holds her instrument to her shoulder, focussed on Maestra Francesca, ready to play. The violoncello player turns to me. 'I am Giuliana,' she whispers, lifting the bow towards the strings.

Maestra Francesca is a commanding presence. She stands still for a moment with the violin bow in the air. She scans the balcony, from the four singers to the far left all the way across the line of eight string players and then along the four singers to her right. She nods at the two soloists standing on either side of her. She looks over our heads to the organist. I lift my instrument to my shoulder. Then she draws her bow down the strings exaggeratedly, and the musicians begin to play. The organ accompanies the string players on the bassline. My instrument sounds softly as I struggle to keep up with the notes. Tonina, I notice, is playing an even line with strong intonation. The soprano standing to Maestra Francesca's left begins to sing, sending a melody across the balcony down into the empty church. We are four lines of parts weaving together in a colourful ribbon of sound, fluttering across the pews and out the back door.

# 3

A few nights later, in the darkness, I stand from my bed and pull the robe over me, half expecting someone to call out. I reach for Maestra Francesca's small leatherbound book of liturgy and clutch it to my side. The only way to finish the day's work is to grasp slivers of night.

I feel my way to the dimly-lit stairs, marked with occasional lamps, towards the music room. I curse my foolish confidence. The music room is pitch dark; it is impossible to find the matches and the candle. I cannot work. Then I hear a clattering in the refectory further down the corridor.

I creep to the refectory. A light glows from the

basement kitchen, revealing spectres of long empty tables. I hold the railing and make my way down the stairs. A wide-set, robed woman is scrubbing a pot with a brush. For a moment, I am lulled by the familiar muffled sound of a pot bumping against a basin under water. I long to be invisible, to stay here, away from the work of my day. To return to what is familiar.

The woman is muttering and then lifting the pot, scouring with the brush. I cough; she spins around, flicking soapsuds across the room.

'I am sorry,' I lower my head.

'You frightened me, that is all. It's Lucietta, isn't it?'

I nod and bite my lip.

She puts the pot on the timber benchtop and dries her hands on her worn apron.

'Sit here,' she says, dragging a chair out from the table. 'I am Suora Teresa. What can I do for you?'

Without warning, I choke back a sob. She gives me a handkerchief, pulling out another chair and sitting opposite me.

'You'll get used to it,' she says. 'Nothing prepares you. Nothing at all. Except convent life itself. Would you like a warm drink?'

I sniff and nod. She limps over to the fireplace where a black pot bubbles. She removes the lid and reaches in a ladle for some hot water to pour into a cup. At the bench, she sprinkles in chamomile leaves and then some cinnamon bark and trickles a spoonful of honey. She smells the liquid and then places it in front of me.

'Let me know if it needs anything,' she says. 'Now. What is that book you are holding?'

I put it down on the table.

'It is the liturgy. I have to learn it, but the days are so busy.'

'Then you must do it now. I also need the nights to catch up. If I do not wash the dishes in the night, we are late with dinner and then supper and so on. It is impossible. So I work at night until it is done. Then I sleep just a little. And then I do it again tomorrow. I think I sometimes sleep while I am serving the supper — but no one has noticed so far. That will help you. Drink it.' She nods towards the cup in my hand.

'The *priora* will not be too pleased to know you are wandering about at night, so make sure you return up there before dawn. I can wake you. I usually just have a doze over there.'

She points to a far wall with a timber bench, a woollen blanket folded neatly upon it.

'So, the advantage of being one of the lowliest servants in the building is — I sleep in the warmest room in the house!' She chuckles to herself and shuffles back to the sink. 'I'm going to finish off now, but you take as long as you need. The light won't bother me either; I could sleep through a battle.'

A flash of black flies across the room, and I jump. She laughs. 'That's Ombra. His job is to catch the mice.'

I crouch down. The cat emerges from the kitchen shadows. A purr rumbles from his throat as he pushes his head into my hand. I run my hands along his spine, and he shivers.

'He also helps clean the plates.'

I sit in the corner, and the cat climbs on my lap immediately, clawing at my thighs. 'Does he ever leave the kitchen?'

'Sometimes. He always comes back, though. Not surprisingly.'

I begin reading the book by the precious lamplight, the cat curled in my lap. Once I start reading the lines, they seem familiar, and I realise I have heard them all in church or in lessons with Padre Porto. They have a lilting cadence; I begin to feel calm.

Suora Teresa places a cushion at one end of the wooden bench, lies down and then draws the blanket up to her chin. Within moments she is snoring, mouth agape.

I find myself humming a tune to remember the phrases. I close my eyes, and the words continue — lines and lines and lines of Latin liturgy running through me like water.

# 4

Wearing my uniform is a kind of disguise: I am both myself and someone else. Maestra Francesca says that the uniform draws eyes to the face. That our souls shine through our countenances, pure and unadulterated by extravagance or ornamentation. Our visages are unsullied by wealth or poverty. The uniform is supposed to free us from worldly concerns. A man can look into my eyes and see what is to be found in me alone without stopping first to consider whether my father was a merchant, money lender or craftsman. Or whether my mother was a fallen woman. Even though it allows our imperfections to be hidden and our exquisite sound to ring out, it occurs to me now that all the covering — the grille, the robes and the wimple — are an invitation for men to stare. A deep discomfort settles inside me.

Regina lends me a small gilded mirror in preparation for my first solo performance in the *sala della musica*. In the early morning, I stare by candlelight at my reflection in the foggy glass, my shining eyes and my wavering features looking as though they would disappear at any moment beneath the sea. I wipe my skin with a wet cloth; it gives me a kind of moist sheen as though I have been caught in a rain shower. I am like a flower emerging from the wet earth. Still, there is an anxious look on my face.

Tonight will be my first solo performance at one of the regular salons for the governing board members and their families. The Porpora Sonata was one of my audition pieces. That day I played it as a solo. This evening, Maestra Francesca will play the basso continuo part on the keyboard. During rehearsal, she is so focussed upon my bowing movement that we are never discernibly out of time. While I have been working towards this performance for many days — perhaps years — I am terrified of failure. The great achievement of musical performance is finding the balance of preparedness. The music must be deeply familiar yet fresh and not over-practised.

'I hated my first solo,' Regina says. 'I was twelve. All I remember was the gasp of shock when the audience first saw my missing arm. It still happens, but I'm used to it now.'

'What happened to your arm?'

'It got caught in a carriage wheel. I don't remember it. Mamma said I was lucky to escape with my life.'

'Are you still nervous before a solo performance?'

'You know, I think it has been trained out of me. Singing the daily offices, mass, other performances and all those musicianship classes when I was younger. I sing more than I speak most days. And, you know, nothing happens if you slip. Maestra Francesca might glare for a moment, but mistakes are quickly forgotten. You are always preparing for the next performance.'

After rest, I walk with Regina downstairs to the courtyard of the four seasons. In the centre, a small, frost-covered garden surrounds the well. Ombra is chasing dry leaves blown by the wind, batting them with his paws. To the right, a second, smaller building is fronted by statues representing the seasons: spring is a carefree girl clutching garlands of flowers. Inside this smaller building, we climb a narrower spiral staircase to the *sala della musica*. We arrive on a small balcony fenced in by a grille of black wrought-iron flowers.

The balcony wall is painted soft white like the inside of an eggshell. There is a decorative grey ribbon painted around the wall as though we are to be presented as gifts. It is as ornate as a picture frame — but what is it framing? I walk across the uneven marble floor towards the grille so I can see out. Below the balcony is an intimate room filled with light. On the far wall is a painting of girls in beautiful gowns — smiling, playing instruments. Behind them, a loosely clad god of music. In front of them, a small greyhound eating biscotti. It is an ethereal image, timeless, beautiful.

'Who are they?' I ask.

Regina laughs. 'It's us. The *coro*.'

I stare at her out of the corner of my eye to see if she is joking. Her countenance is earnest.

'Please take your places,' Maestra Francesca walks towards us and we step away from the grille. We move back towards the wall. Only Giuliana and the other violoncellist have chairs. The rest of us stand around, pressed together in the closed-in space.

'Make sure you can see me!' Maestra Francesca says from her place in front of the grille, looking around and shuffling people sideways with a movement of her hand.

We accompany the singers in Traetta's *Miserere*; the sound is resonant in the confined space. In this echoing acoustic, we sound like a larger group. The parts weave and merge. The sound travels further than we do. Will it be discerned in the *calle* outside? Maestra Francesca occasionally glares at one of us when there is a slip in tuning or intonation, but she does not spend a lot of time on corrections.

'Please go over anything you think needs work. And then rest this afternoon, so you are fresh this evening,' she says, putting her papers on the stand and leaving it pushed up against the grille before walking out the door and descending the stairs.

As soon as she is gone, Giuliana says, 'Come on, let's have a look at the *sala della musica*!'

We leave our instruments in their cases and step through the door in the side wall, circling back down the narrow spiral staircase to the room below. It has tall windows and soft lace curtains. It is like a small ballroom, a refined and colourful space that I would expect to see in a palazzo. Around the edges are undersized furnishings: small velvet-covered stools and narrow gilded tables that will later be laden with food. I look closely at the mural on the wall in front of me. The girls have soft round faces, pale and plump shoulders. The silk gowns flow around them. Giuliana and one of the other girls, Agata, who has a purple birthmark on her cheek, link arms and do a kind of peasant dance across the pink marble floor. Regina vocalises high in her soprano range; it floats in the air like birdsong.

We return to the balcony that evening, arriving

early to tune our instruments. We have been given lace collars to wear for the performance. The threads make my neck itch. From the balcony, we watch a small audience gathering below. Scents of lavender and rose mingle. People turn to speak with their friends and relatives; men look distractedly in our direction. From this vantage, it is as though the people below are the spectacle — ladies in rustling silk: burgundy, green and navy, the beautiful girls of the painter's imagination on the wall behind them. Servants appear with platters of tiny morsels — battered shellfish and sweetmeats — with goblets of deep red liquid, moving slowly around the room. I feel as though I have arrived in my life. I am a working musician, moving among people with breeding and education and appreciation for finery. Distilled fragrances and the sweetness of wine mask the city's salty undercurrent. Lamplight reflects the brightness off the walls. And while my eyes are drawn to the generous light and the colour below, in the cramped balcony the light is grey. Maestra Francesca stands in position with her violin, signalling for us to take our places. Then she cuts through the air with her bow, and we begin. My sound is stronger now. Tonight, I am keeping up; I am a vital part of the ensemble. The audience below does not fall silent. There is a kind of mumbling below as we play.

Maestra Francesca plays and conducts by a single

lamp. It is difficult to make out the notes on the page, but my fingers remember where to go. It is a harmonious sound; I peer through the grille at the men and women craning their necks to see us. The grille is there to mask our physical imperfections: no matter our appearance, we always sound angelic.

When we finish, there is generous applause. An old man calls, 'Brava! Brava!' Servants with trays move around downstairs, and then Maestra Francesca nods to Agata and Regina for their duet. The three of them leave the balcony to make their way into the room for their performance. As soon as they are gone, the rest of us move to the bars so we can peer through. Agata and Regina are standing next to Maestra Francesca, seated at a spinet in the *sala della musica*. It is a fine gilded instrument with ivory keys, the timber surface painted with cherubs. The audience is standing around them in a kind of semicircle, close. The room hums with chatter and glasses clinking; the smell of fresh cake wafts towards us.

Maestra Francesca nods her head, and the girls stand rigidly — hands by their sides. Her playing is somewhat deliberate and plodding, but I can see now that she has transferred her conducting to both hands and her faintly nodding head; she is intent on controlling the music. Agata inclines her head towards Maestra Francesca and begins to sing. Now, she clasps her hands before her, opens her mouth slightly. And then the sound reaches my ears, mellow and rich, the voice of a much larger girl. The sound swells in the room. Regina then begins to sing, her voice high and bell-like. All three of them sway with the melody, looking at each other. Regina's missing arm is barely noticeable, the sleeve draped at her side.

The song finishes, and the girls bow. The colour has risen in Agata's cheeks, disguising the blemish on her cheek. Francesca leads them from the room. Servants begin walking around again with trays. Guests take food in their fingers and sip their wine. On the balcony above, I clutch my instrument and sheet music in sweaty hands. I make my way out towards the staircase, meeting Maestra Francesca on the stairs.

'Are you ready?'

I nod.

On the landing outside the *sala della musica*, the air is cooler. I wipe each hand on my robes and stand still for a moment. My body twitches with an excited kind of energy. Part of me longs to run. But I know I cannot. I have been preparing for this performance. My instrument would be expanding and contracting in microscopic degrees in the changing temperature, detectable only through sound. I attempt to tune it out there in the stairwell, notes bouncing off the stonework.

I walk into the room, carrying the sheet music at my side. People are standing around in small groups, watching me. A man in a dark woollen cape turns and stares at me. I look away. Another man with dark hair and a green cloak is standing with a shorter older man. Staring. And nearby, a seated older lady with a carved wooden cane, wearing a navy blue gown. Sipping from a crystal tumbler.

I place the music on the stand. Maestra Francesca is sitting on the spinet stool, her hands clasped in her lap. I try not to look up towards the balcony where I know the *coro* is watching. Some of the girls would be awaiting my triumphant success. Others longing for my failure so that they can step into my place. As though I have never been. All holding their breath.

I know my music is all I have. It is the one gift that will carry me from one place to another. If not for the music, Mamma said, I would have married a fisherman at the earliest possible moment and would perhaps already be carrying my second child. And it would keep going in this way until I perhaps died in childbirth like Signora Giuseppina next door.

There is the music, but there is also the fear — always — that it will go. One day I will wake, and my fingers will no longer move. Or my shoulders will ache so much that I can no longer hold a violin.

I play because it is a need: a deep driving force — like the need to eat. Sometimes the food is bland

and tasteless, but I must keep eating to remain alive. I can spend hours practising, and sometimes my mind is so vacant, so absent from itself, that it is as though I have been sitting in a room by myself doing nothing but breathe. And I have not been conscious of any breath at all.

But I cannot trust a performance to such vacancy. I cannot trust my fingers and arms and even my feet to undertake the correct minutiae of movement, to ensure the pitch of every note. And so, I come to myself in those final moments before the performance, confronted with the terrifying reality of what I must do.

Now, I hold my instrument aloft, bowing arm raised. Maestra Francesca meets my eye. I nod, and she begins playing the introduction on the spinet with the exaggerated motion she uses when leading. All the time she is playing, she is watching my face and not her fingers. The music is within her. She is slowing slightly for my entry. For some moments, my music is swallowed by the din of chattering people. And then it soars over them. One by one, they stop talking.

What an enormous undertaking it is, finally, that moment of being completely present, of standing exposed before an audience who is free to look at me and think what it likes. I cannot control the thoughts of the spectators. Or the images in their minds.

I am in the *sala della musica*, standing in front of a glorious mural of girls playing in elegant gowns and a small greyhound eating a biscotto.

When I stand in front of the mural, I have to imagine that all those well-dressed and perfumed spectators with their goblets and sweetmeats are not staring at me but at the paintings. I keep my eyes on the music before me even though I am not reading it; I am hiding behind it, as though it, too, is a gilded bar or a painting that takes up a whole wall. I am gazing at the strange brown notes that move like ants across the parchment, thinking about the remarkable fact that humans have learned to notate sound.

Now I am swimming inside the music, hearing every note, seeing the patterns on the page, but blocking out the audience. I cannot bear it.

I have been inhabiting Porpora's sonata for days. It has been occupying me. It moved around my mind while I ate or dressed. I had to push it aside at times to perform at mass or play at vespers. It played over and over while I slept.

This state of absence is not death, but I fear it is not entirely life, either. I am floating, drifting, somewhere in between. At the back of the room, I spot the *priora* swaying slightly to the music. And the room is hot now, as though fire burns within it.

My sonata is drawing to a close. My right hand is

deliberate and steady as my left hand gently moves in a wide vibrato. I am returning to the present in the *sala della musica* with the audience and its scented clothes, an unpalatable mixture of sweet and sour and very salty. I finish playing, and the final note lingers for a moment in the air.

Suddenly, there is applause, and I am bowing — and then I am relieved to feel my feet firmly in their shoes, solidly on the ground. I smile; my cheeks heat. The young man in the green cloak is staring intently at me. I bow again, mainly to remove myself from his gaze. But when I raise my head, he is still there, so I begin to gather my parchment, tucking the instrument under my arm.

I push past gowns of silk and satin and lace and wool. I am scratched on the arm by the gem upon a lady's finger. Maestra Francesca stands to the side, holding out an arm to usher me away from the audience. She smiles at me and nods. Her mouth forms a word: lovely. I try to smile back, but my lips are tight. They cannot move at all. My feet also feel stiff as I trudge from the room. Maestra Francesca holds the door open for me. I am out once more in the draughty stairwell. For a moment, I entered a new world, beautiful, enchanting and mysterious. But now it is behind me. I left my music behind. In all senses. Do the sounds of my instrument linger still? Are the guests swallowing it with their sweetmeats?

The other girls are out on the landing. They pat my arm and say, that was beautiful, perfect, well done. I nod and try to smile, but now the top of my scalp is buzzing, and I am perspiring.

'Lucietta,' Maestra Francesca's head is bent towards me.

'What is it?'

'Since this is your first performance, there are people who would like to meet you,' Maestra Francesca says. I want to refuse, but she is not asking me.

'Yes, Maestra.' My legs are weakening now, aching, and I am not sure how much longer they will be able to hold me up.

The case feels heavier than usual, the clasp stiff and rusting. Agata reaches out her hand and takes my instrument. The girls return to the balcony. For a moment, I imagine Maestra Francesca has gone, and I can also leave, taking the steps two at a time to the dormitory. But she is there, holding out her arm as though ready to lead me. She takes me by the hand, and I imagine I must look as feverish and weakened as I have come to feel.

Inside the *sala della musica*, most of the audience is standing, apart from the elderly woman in the navy blue gown sitting in the front row, speaking with Padre, the priest.

Maestra Francesca leads me towards an older

man and woman standing with the young man who was staring at me as I played.

'Excuse me,' Maestra Francesca says. 'Don Leonardi. Our new musician Lucietta.'

The elderly man takes my hand; it is cold and sweaty, and I long to take it back. But he lifts it to his lips, eyes sparkling.

I curtsey as low as I can manage. I am beginning to feel dizzy.

'Our son, Don Leonardi the younger,' the woman says. She is wearing a fat powdered wig high upon her head. She is pale, her eyes grey. The man wears his long, forest-green cloak above white stockings and buckled black shoes. I nod my head, and he does the same.

'Lovely playing,' he says. 'I learned for a while, but I did not have any ability.'

'He sounded like a cat having its tail pulled,' his mother says.

'I think that is quite usual,' I say. 'For the first two years. It can take time to tame a violin.'

'I would say yours is quite tame now,' Don Leonardi says. 'It obeys your every whim.'

'It's just practice.' I stare down at my feet. My toes are lumpy in their shoes. 'Anyone can play if they practise.'

'Not as well as you, my dear,' the lady sips her wine.

I raise my eyes. I think about leaving. And then the room spins. Maestra Francesca grabs my arm hard. 'Our musicians need to rest now,' she says, pulling me away, leading me from the swaying room.

'What is the matter?' she asks as we step onto the landing and descend to the foyer.

'I feel unwell.'

'Sit down,' she says. 'I will bring you some water.'

I sit on a stool. The liquid is sharp and sweet. I lean my head on my palms.

'Come, Lucietta,' Maestra Francesca says, taking the cup. 'Let me take you upstairs. Can you eat something?'

'I am not sure.'

She disappears upstairs for a moment and returns with a saucer full of sweetmeats. They are colourful and glazed, covered in fruit and nuts.

'You know that there have been several marriages between the musicians here and young men in the audience.'

My body stiffens.

'It happens quickly sometimes. Girls attract attention soon after they arrive. There is a desire, in some noble families, for the young men to marry educated women. Young women who have been too busy studying to become too — worldly. Give it some thought, Lucietta. It could be a wonderful opportunity for you.' I look at her in surprise. It is less than two weeks since I arrived.

My knees tremble as I climb the staircase. I finally reach the dormitory, and I allow myself to collapse on the bed. I eat one of the sweetmeats in small bites. It has been a long time since I ate. I cannot recall when it was. I place the saucer on my chest of drawers and lower myself down to the pillow.

I pull the stiff covers right up over my head and roll on my side. The air is grey and dim. Footsteps and voices echo in the building below. The music starts up again in my mind, and I allow it to absorb me as though it is a kind of lullaby. My hands imagine they are playing, the sound continues.

The next day, I sleep a little longer than usual; there is no need for early morning practice. Now that I have performed solo, I am less afraid of playing with the *coro*. It is a relief to play in a group, to be invisible.

The violin has defined my life. When I was young, it separated me from every other child I knew. It was a constant reminder that there were aspects of my life that remained secret. And yet I loved it, was drawn to it, enjoyed the sound I could make that was not made by other children who lived in the *calle*.

It was the violin and the person behind it, my father, the mysterious puppeteer who controls my life from afar, who brought me here. Without his manoeuvring, I would be washing Lionello's socks in a metal basin of brown water, tipping the water out onto the street to either avoid or land upon the most irritating of the children next door.

The violin taunts me to play it at all hours. It was my invitation to the balcony in the Derelitti, to the *sala della musica*. When I lift this small wooden box to my face, I can smell fish the way Mamma used to prepare it: salted and fried in our room until it was soft enough to eat with just a fork. It would flake and soften upon the tongue. The box still carries with it these remnants from home.

This building is cavernous, and there are walls to separate the spheres of life. The violin does not come with me to where food is prepared and eaten. It does not have the opportunity to become infused with the scent of marinated vegetables or eggs. These foods and this life will perhaps leave no trace. If I go elsewhere, will I be reaching deep into my memory to revive this time? It may leave no evidence that it ever existed, and — in time — I might come to doubt my recollections. The violin is my key to this life. Are there other doors that my key would unlock?

# 5

A day later at supper, I tear corners off my bread, chewing slowly until Agata taps my shoulder. I look up.

'Maestra Francesca asked me to find you. There is someone to see you in the foyer.'

'Who is it?'

I have been here long enough to know that it is not visiting hour and that Maestra Francesca is generally observant of the rules. I put the last corner of bread in my mouth and chew as I stand.

'I'll take that,' Agata removes the plate from my hands. 'You should go.'

The building is bathed in soft winter light.

The lack of cloud brings a chill to the air. I stride through the building, shadowed by the cat. I hear voices as I near the foyer. Once there, I see Maestra Francesca on the other side of the grille speaking with a man, free to leave if she should so choose. The man is thin; he wears a familiar green cloak. He has dark hair and nods as he speaks. As I near the wrought-iron bars, he smiles at me. He reveals neat white teeth. I have rarely in my life seen such teeth. They shine like pearls. And the man displays them often as though he is proud of them. They have perhaps required almost as much time as the perfecting of an instrument to maintain to such a standard. I choose one of the timber seats opposite the grate and sit down. It is like being locked in prison staring out.

'You remember Don Leonardi,' Maestra Francesca is looking at me strangely from the other side of the grille.

I nod.

'Please sit down,' she pulls a chair closer to him, and he brings it right up to the bars before sitting on it. We are sitting opposite each other now, separated by the grille. And while I can see Maestra Francesca longs to stay, she moves back and seats herself at the desk where she opens the ledger. I cannot help feeling uneasy that they have the freedom to come and go. They are both free to observe me while I am behind the bars that appear like a cage.

And Maestra Francesca will, I know, eventually unlock the door and farewell him. He will leave. And I will stay. Is she encouraging him to take me away? Does she want to be rid of me so soon after I have arrived?

She has her head down now, bent over the ledger while she writes carefully with her quill.

'How are you feeling today?' Don Leonardi asks me.

'I am quite well. And you?'

'Quite well also. I did enjoy the recital.'

'Thank you.'

Despite the cold, Don Leonardi's face has a brightness. He seems to glow in the lamplight. From such proximity, I become aware that his skin is not entirely smooth; it is etched with tiny craters.

'How long have you been playing?'

'Many years. I do not remember ever not playing. I think I was four when they gave me my first violin.'

'Who gave it to you?'

I am silent for a moment.

'My parents.'

I know I should ask him something, give him something to discuss. But I am not skilled in the art of conversation. I am not trained in the acceptable lines of inquiry of a man such as this.

'You enjoy music, then?' I ask.

'My sister plays the spinet rather well. I miss hearing it now that she is married.'

I nod. There is silence. I hear Maestra Francesca's quill moving across the parchment. Somewhere behind me, a dripping sound echoes. Voices pass by in the street outside. Then they are gone. I stare at my hands. Maestra Francesca stops writing and looks up. She stands, and her chair drags across the marble floor. Don Leonardi stands too. He rubs his fingers together.

'I must go,' he says.

'Thank you for coming,' Maestra Francesca says. She is looking at me now, and I am sitting on my chair as though watching a performance. She inclines her head towards me slightly, and I remember myself. I stand.

'Yes, thank you,' I say. He bends over so that the distance between us reduces. He reaches a hand towards the grille and then takes it back and rubs it with his other hand.

'I will come again,' he says, 'when I can.'

'Visiting hour is generally on a Sunday afternoon,' Maestra Francesca says, 'After two. The *priora* is reluctant to allow visitors at other times.'

'I see. Well, thank you.'

He nods and turns away from me.

'Goodbye,' I say. And he turns back, smiles for a moment, and then allows Maestra Francesca to escort him to the door. The cold air creeps towards me.

I turn back, relieved at the safety of my enclosure. I stride quickly back through the passageway into the building. I cannot bear to be there a moment longer. I do not want to hear what Maestra Francesca might say.

I climb the stairs. It is rest time. Agata and Regina are sitting on Regina's bed; one of the girls is reading from a small book. Tonina is standing in front of the open wardrobe, staring in as though looking for something.

I sit down on my bed and take out a sheet of music. I read it at the correct tempo, the notes sounding in my mind.

'Who was it?' Agata says. 'Who was your visitor?'

'Oh.' I smile and look down at the parchment before meeting her eye. 'Don Leonardi. He was at the recital yesterday.'

'And he came back? So soon?'

I nod, growing hot.

'What was it like having a man come and visit you?'

I think for a moment of the stilted conversation. The darkness. The cold. The bars.

'He has very nice teeth,' I say.

'Was it hard to find something to talk about?'

I smile. 'A little. It was a short conversation.'

I stare at my hands. Agata laughs. 'Did he say that he would come back?'

'Yes.'

'I suppose you could think about suitable topics of conversation. Do you know any, Regina?'

'What would I know about speaking to men?' Regina says, 'I don't think I will ever need to know.'

'We have our music, though,' Agata says. 'Not every girl must marry.'

'Maddalena had a young man visit after she performed in the *sala della musica*. She said he had been in the navy, and he recounted fascinating tales of his voyages. He came often and eventually petitioned for her hand. They gave it to him after a while. He was very persistent.'

'She really wanted to go, though.' Agata says. 'She could not wait to leave.'

'Who wouldn't want to go and live with someone who told stories of other places!'

'I think I'd prefer to give concerts, actually,' Agata says. 'I mean, who's to say that he remained in Venice after they were married? He might have gone back to sea.'

'I wouldn't mind that,' Regina says. 'Living alone in a palazzo.'

—

When I close my eyes to sleep, it is not his teeth I

see but his eyes. They are so dark they are almost black. He does not seem of this world. I can admire him, but that is all. I cannot imagine spending time with him. The thought of him reaching out a hand towards me frightens me. What would he do if I went with him? And while part of me longs to be in a house that might have air and light, part of me is frightened of a life away from music and people. A life where I might not understand the rules.

# 6

There are moments when you cannot forget that you were raised by a woman who is not your mother. To be loved is not the same as to belong. I have spent my life searching for a place of belonging.

A few years ago, I sat at the kitchen table in the semi-darkness, trying to complete a composition for Padre Porto. The ink was barely visible in the smoky glow, and I was bent over my parchment, fingers gripping the quill tightly. I appraised my curling, sloping script. Lionello sat next to me and began to slurp his broth from a chipped ceramic bowl.

'What are you doing?' he asked.

'Working.' I did not lift my head but remained focussed upon the page.

'Let me see,' He leaned over towards me. And then suddenly, he reached out a hand and knocked the ink bottle. The rust-coloured ink bled profusely, rivulets of brown flowing slowly across the parchment towards the table's edge.

'Lionello!' I screamed as tears sprang to my eyes.

'Sorry, sorry!' he was clutching at handkerchiefs, blotting with washcloths, suddenly moving at twice his usual speed, his cheeks growing crimson.

'How could you! You great oaf!'

'Lucietta!' Mamma scolded from the fireside where she was hanging damp clothes. 'It was an accident. He has apologised.'

'But you don't understand. I have to start all over again. My page is ruined now. That took — hours.'

'It will be all the better for the practice.'

'No. That was my very best. I can't do better.'

I got up from the table and ran outside, slamming the door behind me. I ran along the cobblestones, stumbling through alleyways, over bridges, right to the edge of the island. I slowed as Santi Giovanni e Paolo came into relief. I continued past the washerwomen, past their sheets hanging in the salty air, along the canal — past the Mendicanti to the bollards at the Fondamente Nove. Venice was wholly inhabited. Men had paved over the sand to its very edges.

The *ponente* blew from the west. I stared across

the choppy green sea towards San Michele. Even this had been overrun by humans, stolen from nature, walled and built over with its church and convent. My breathing steadied as I closed my eyes. I tried to remember my birth mother's face. How could I have forgotten her? Her voice. Her touch. I tried to conjure her from the depths of my memory, but could not. I felt as though I were scratching the very depths of my mind until it bled — the image I sought was completely erased. It was as though she had never been.

But clearly, she had been, or I would not exist. And she had carried me within her. I imagined her love. I imagined her touch, her soft words to me as a baby. Surely there had been love? Mamma had assured me that the shame of my birth could be wiped away by God and a church education. But my soul was blackened by my mother having a child out of wedlock. The stain was responsible for my existence; it had given me life.

I stared across the water towards the red brick wall and arched entrance way to San Michele. Perhaps I was like my mother in some way. Maybe we had the same brown eyes or the same crooked front teeth or the same voice. I was like some kind of window reflecting an earlier version of her.

The thought of my birth mother was entwined with my desire for belonging. Without her, I would always be an outsider, held at a certain distance by Mamma and Papà even though I did not doubt their love. I was being educated above my station, yet because Mamma had spared me so much daily work, it would be difficult for me to live comfortably within the class I had been raised. My education held me apart from the other girls I shared shellfish broth with in the neighbourhood. I was tolerated as an eccentric playfellow by Lionello's friends as I lifted my ill-fitting boots from under my pinafore to kick a hand-sewn ball high into the air. There was nothing like that moment: being responsible for the flight of an object, setting it loose where pigeons and seagulls fluttered and insects flew. I would watch the boys — pushing each other, hands in the air, eyes fixed on the ball — not realising they were treading on each other's feet and on the fish bones that had been dropped by startled cats.

The waves lapped at the embankment so that I did not hear him at first. Then — the regular splashing of oars.

'Lucietta!' Pietro was in his fishing shirt and trousers, rowing his *barca*. 'Would you like to come on board?' he stepped off the vessel to tie the rope to the bollard.

I stepped shakily to the *barca* and sat, staring out to sea. The clouds were growing grey now.

'Who was my real mother?' I asked.

'We do not know for certain. She left you at
the Pietà. Out of circumstance, I know that. Not
because you were unwanted. I am grateful.'

'Why?'

'Because she gave us a gift. A blessing you are in
our lives.'

He untied the vessel and began to ease her out
into the water.

'How do you know she is dead?'

For some moments, Pietro let the vessel bob up
and down on the waves. He stared towards San
Michele.

'It is your father. We do not know who he is, but
he keeps an eye on things, as you know.'

'Can I not go to him?'

'It is possible . . . he may one day make himself
known to you. But he has arranged things in such
a way that it is impossible to find him. I have tried.'

'You tried?'

'When you were three. You raged for several days
in a fever. We thought — we thought we might lose
you. Silvia did not know what to do. I don't think
she slept for a week, so busy was she with flannels
and poultices and sending for a nurse with leeches.
I went to the Pietà. Begged them to find him, to see
if he could help in some way.

After four days, you were weak, but the fever
had passed. You were sitting up, sucking on some

pomegranate seeds. A messenger arrived. He claimed to be from your father. Said he was not currently in Venice but that he hoped you would make a full recovery. He said your mother had passed away. He brought with him a basket of milk, eggs and chocolate.'

'Chocolate?'

'Yes. We had never tried it before, and we did not because it was for you. But the smell was — glorious.'

'Where do you think my mother is buried?'

'I cannot know that, Lucietta.'

'Will you take me to San Michele?' Papà nodded and changed direction away from Venice.

I longed to leave the city, to sit under a tree and empty my mind of thoughts. The island across the water, visible from the Fondamente Nove, was a place we had visited during my childhood. I remembered spending the afternoon playing hide and seek around the monastery garden with Lionello. The current was stronger as we moved into the Canale de le Nove. Pietro grimaced with the exertion. His oars pulled through the water; the *barca* pitched towards the island. When we arrived, Pietro threw his rope over a bollard, and the boat rocked. I stood and allowed him to help me onto dry land. A large gull with a hooked beak watched as Pietro anchored his boat.

We walked across stone to the open gate. From here, I stepped into a garden. The path was rimmed with lavender. To my right was an orchard of fruit trees in fresh blossom, humming with bees. The convent courtyard was towards my left. In it was a vegetable garden with newly planted seedlings. A nun crouched over one of its corners, her hands in the earth. She did not seem to notice our presence.

'Just let me know when you're ready to leave,' he said.

I stepped carefully among the stones. The island was divided into different areas. There were places where nature was fighting to take hold: calendula blossomed while rosemary pushed spiky leaves up among the stones.

Past the fruit trees was a large patch of earth where wildflowers grew in orange, red and yellow. A single tree grew, encircled by a small grassy meadow. Had this patch of green once been a burial ground? I sat beneath the tree and leaned up against its gnarled bark. I closed my eyes and tried to sense my birth mother's presence nearby. But instead, I saw Silvia in my mind's eye, slicing at a firm fish with the blunt paring knife, spooning last week's lard into the pan over the cooking fire. I felt her hands tugging at my hair, tying it in place. I saw her smile as she greeted me in the morning.

I would always regret not knowing my mother,

for without her, a crucial link was missing. Knowing her would not have guaranteed anything at all. Love, belonging, wholeness. These were slippery sentiments that might not come from a single person.

I stood underneath the tree and untied the ribbon from my hair, letting the wind caress my locks and set them free. Of course, I had imagined that my mother was from one of the noble families written down in the Golden Book. The youngest daughter, the one with no marriage dowry, committed to a convent by her parents: in love with a boy from a neighbouring palazzo. I had lain awake at night and tried to picture her: long dark hair, working hard at her spinet or violin. I imagined that perhaps my affinity for music grew before my birth, that watery melodies came to me from the moment I could first hear, to the beat of my mother's heart. But if I am honest, I know this is fiction. In reality, my mother was probably low-born.

I have wondered whether it is better to be certain or better to retain the mystery. Would I want to know my mother, no matter who she was? And the answer is, without a doubt, that I would. I would not want to be beholden to her if she had slipped below the level of respectability. But I would want to know who she was, even if it only served to increase my gratitude for my own life. Life was like broth: in it, we would find rich nourishing food along with the dried herbs and shrivelled carrots from the bottom of the cupboard — as well as the stale bread that had lost its flavour and goodness but helped to fill the void.

I stared down the hill to where Pietro lay upon the grass, mouth ajar, snoring. I walked towards him.

# 7

The air in the dormitory is heavy with sighing girls. The thin curtain allows the light through and illuminates the shadow girls in the moonlight. They lie in varied positions: Tonina in a jumble of blankets. Agata neatly on her side. Regina on her stomach. How beautiful they are in their repose. But I am wide awake. A Pampani violin sonata, a virtuosic piece found recently in the Derelitti archives, is loud in my ears, my fingers twitching. I need to practise. I swing my legs over the bed and find my slippers. I lift my cloak over my nightdress. I fumble under the bed for my instrument. The clasp opens with a loud click, and I pause for a moment. Someone groans; someone rolls over. I hurriedly pull my cloak and wimple on, lifting the instrument case and moving towards the doorway. In the corridor, a single lamp shines. I slide my hand down the bannisters as I make my way downstairs.

The building is weightless with spirits resting. In the night, I feel it has more space for me. As I near the music room, a figure moves towards me. I freeze and stand still against the wall. It is the *priora*, clutching a book to her chest. She stares straight ahead and does not see me.

I step away from the wall and continue to the music room. The chairs are in a semicircle from an earlier rehearsal, the sounds long extinguished from the air. A room that held wine has a faintly discernible scent of fermented grapes. Will a music room always hold traces of music? Once the instruments, the pages and the musicians are gone, will there be evidence of the room's purpose to someone passing through later? Will there ever come a time where such a room might have a different purpose?

I feel for the desk and reach into the drawer for the matches I know to be hidden there. I set the candle alight. I close the door firmly. I hope that the walls will hold the secret of my night time playing, for I am uneasy now. What if I am discovered?

The cold air in the music room slides under my clothes and chills my skin. My fingers are stiff, and

I am not sure I will be able to play. I am grateful for my cropped hair and my wimple for it stands as a barrier between my body and what feels like the quiet chill before a snowstorm. I am beginning to long for the warmth of my bed and regret coming here tonight. I hold my fingers before the candle. My hands make giant shadows on the walls, like the monsters in the stories Papà used to tell Lionello at night when he thought I was asleep.

The blood is just warmed enough to return movement to my fingers. The score is faintly visible on my music stand. I am afraid someone will discover me here practising in the night, that I will wake some of the nuns, and I know they do not like being woken. So, in the end, I practise with the fingers of each hand and the lightest bow I have ever used, a bow that only occasionally strikes a string by accident, creating a quiet hum of sound. But I am committing my Pampani sonata to memory, its fast passages trilling in my mind. Despite my nerves, I am excited at the freedom that comes with having the music room to myself, not being interrupted, not having to sign in or sign out, or plan rehearsals a week ahead. I close my eyes, and my fingers angle the bow, silently holding it just above the strings. In my mind, I hear a glorious sound. I send the music out behind the drifting curtain, out through the bevelled glass window where it dips and dives over the water and then floats across the city.

I am animated but also worn out. I quietly place my instrument back in its case. I am careful to extinguish the candle. And then, suddenly, I hear footsteps. I look around quickly and find a corner in which to crouch. The footsteps draw nearer, and the door creaks open. Out of the corner of my eye, I see a candle flame illuminating the shadows. I hear a throat clear. It is the *priora*. I hold my breath. Eventually, she turns away and leaves the room.

I sit trembling for some minutes, holding my instrument in my arms. It is not quite animate — it brings me comfort and reassurance, made of once living things, made to sing like a living thing. Then my breathing slows; my mind drifts. I become aware of slightly flickering light: clouds drifting before the moon and then away. I stand and wobble for a moment before summoning the strength to return to the dormitory.

I creep back to my bed and return the instrument to its place underneath. I lift back the blanket and place my hand on the sheet. The blankets have retained my body warmth as though I never left.

# 8

After the coro rehearsal, I practise the regular parts of the sung mass alone in the music room. They are simple melodies, but there are so many — and I need to know them by heart. I play each section first studying the music and then with my eyes closed. I worry that I will play the wrong part of the mass at the wrong time. I have a fear of flying with nowhere to land. Of soaring away from the group. Of committing a great and audible error. Of losing my place. In my mind, I am singing the liturgy as I have heard now, day after day. I do not know how many days. Time is blurring.

Until I came here three weeks ago, I had only

heard my own playing and the occasional demonstration from Don Domenico. His bow stroke was always firmer, had greater control. In this school, with all these new pieces to learn and strict rules, I am beginning to doubt my ability to follow so many threads at the same time. To remember the words and the associated melody — perfect the sound, watch the conductor, listen to what is happening around me: the words, the music, the sounds of women singing. Breathing. Muttering. Whispering. Do not ever lag. Anticipate, but do not allow a soft hum to strike. Keep the bow away from the strings except when they must connect, and then do it with strength and surety. It is a terrifying enterprise.

The elation — when it succeeds — is unlike anything I have known. The satisfaction when Maestra Francesca nods at me and smiles is like a burst of the sweetest fruit in my mouth. It is like the lagoon on a summer's day, the gentle breeze playing with the flowing hair in my memory.

One afternoon at the end of rehearsal, Maestra Francesca motions to me to wait. The other girls gather their instruments and papers, glance at me for a moment and then step from the room. They huddle together, whispering. Maestra Francesca beckons me closer.

'It is usual for musicians like you to take on some teaching here. The *priora* suggested you might like to teach Tonina. She is eight years old. She has been here since she was five. She is very gifted.'

'Teach?'

'Yes. It is part of your training. Have you taught before?'

I shake my head. How could I have taught before? What child in my neighbourhood living with her natural parents would have had access to a violin?

'We can help you. Provide music. Advice.'

She raises her eyebrows at the word 'advice', and I realise that I will never ask it of her. I do not want her to know all that I do not know.

'Tonina usually has her lessons in the morning after terce on Mondays, Tuesdays and Thursdays. I am very busy at this time, with the music program, and this might be valuable training for you both. This is how we create such outstanding musicians here, giving them lessons three times a week, training them to teach as soon as they are able and old enough. Do you have any questions?' Later, I will regret that I did not ask how one fills in so much lesson time. Although I have been taught for as long as I can remember, I do not know how to teach. I have never thought about the how only the what. Of course, my teachers demonstrated technique and critiqued my posture and tuning. Don Domenico brought the life of the streets, the world of men, into my lessons with his talk of meetings in coffee houses and the concerts he had attended. Is there a way to be a different teacher? As a girl, perhaps I can impart more than notes and technique. Perhaps I can teach her how to apply herself to music with the same fervour that many women apply to domestic life.

As I shake my head, she says, 'You should know — Tonina can play anything she has heard. Her aural memory is unlike anything I have ever come across. Her reading is slower. I minimise demonstrating. It takes her longer to learn music through reading, but it is an important investment.'

—

The knock at the rehearsal room door is a quiet tapping, as though it does not want to be heard.

'Come in!' I call, but the tapping continues, and I wonder whether the heavy stone walls, the oak door, the high ceiling are so impenetrable that they lock in the sound.

I return my instrument and bow to the case and step to the door, pulling it open. Tonina stands there looking down at her feet. There are some darker patches down her front, spilled hardened food. She is gripping her instrument case in front of her like some kind of shield. It is battered and worn, the timber polished but marked with scratches.

I stand back to allow her to enter. She steps

inside, moves to the corner, and releases her instrument and its bow. I reach to tune the violin, but she is already standing there, in position with her eyes closed, plucking, drawing the bow, tightening to adjust, making it sound again, the whole procedure complete in a few seconds.

She is still staring at her feet. I sit down on the spinet stool, facing away from the keyboard. Our heads are a similar height now.

'Hello, Tonina. Would you like to play me something?'

My voice echoes for a moment and then is swallowed by air. She does not speak. She does not move. It is difficult to keep myself still and silent. I have a natural yearning to fill the silence.

She lifts the bow. The beat is already pulsing inside her petite frame, and she catches it like a child skipping. She begins to play a rapid sonata. The passages are in tune, as accurate as a newly tuned harpsichord. The tiny fingertips on the half-sized instrument are precisely placed, creating a professional flurry of sound.

And when she finishes, she stands still for a moment while the sound floats around the room. Her body is trembling. She is staring at the wall.

'Tonina, that was wonderful!' I stand, and she steps back, looking at me but for a moment. I sit back down.

She does not speak. How can I teach her? What can I teach her? 'How long have you been playing that piece?'

I am beginning to feel foolish now, as though I am talking to myself. 'Tonina, what would you like to work on in your lessons?'

I wait until I can no longer bear the silence.

'Can you play for me the technical work you have been doing?'

It is a Tessarini trattimento, one I recognise. I ask her to slow it down, and she plays it at half speed. Occasionally the tuning slips. This is one weakness, then. I make her play the piece slowly again and stop her after two bars.

'Again. Very slowly, watch the tuning.'

She purses her lips. Her eyes are far away. The sound now is a little wavering, less confident. Am I frightening her? I long to know how she was taught before. If I cannot become a good teacher, is there a life for me as a musician? It would be impossible to reinvent myself as an ordinary girl without music.

She has been here only minutes, but I do not know how to proceed. In my lessons, there was sometimes conversation about matters other than music. But this child will not speak. I want to give her some kind of gift, something to show my good intention. Something to allow us to forget, for a moment, our designated roles. I reach into my robes.

I have kept the small thin ribbon Mamma used to tie my hair that final morning before leaving home.

It is a small white scrap of silk. I hand it to the child. She stares at her palm for a moment. Then she pushes it into a side pocket, which I can see is already bulging with found items. A hardened wax seal falls out and skips across the tiles.

She turns away, pushes the violin back into its case with the bow. As she leaves the room, the case hits the door, and the sound echoes around the corridor. I step outside the music room and watch her running, head down, arms swinging, case occasionally hitting the wall as she moves away from me as fast as she can. I feel a profound sense of failure that I could not keep her with me. I could not divert the child even for half an hour.

In the night, it is hard to sleep. I do not know the best way to make Tonina speak, and how can I teach a silent child? Without words, she is unable to guide me to help her. The following day, I watch her in the refectory and see that she is withdrawn and silent among the other children. In rehearsal, Maestra Francesca does not speak to her but seems to communicate with her eyes.

———

In the refectory after supper two days later, I slip down the stairs to the kitchen. Suora Teresa is slicing oranges into glistening wheels. She nods towards a plate of biscotti by way of greeting. I lift one to my mouth and take a bite. The almonds are freshly roasted. They are smooth as bone; they crunch loudly as I bite down.

'Did you see my niece, Agata, today?' she asks.

I nod.

'Take her some biscotti. Tell her to visit soon. She always loved my biscotti. When she was small, her parents used to bring her to visit, and she took handfuls of biscotti home in her pockets.'

After compline, I meet Agata in one of the smaller music rooms. By candlelight, she is copying lines from a large musical score. I lean over the page.

'How can you see that?' I ask as the shadows loom over the parchment.

'You get used to working by candlelight. Normally I try to work during the day, but this is urgent, so I have to finish it tonight.'

'Did Maestra Francesca ask you to copy it?'

'Yes. I've been a copyist for the last year. It's quite well paid. I have to concentrate very closely so the copies are accurate.'

I reach into my pocket for the wrapped package. 'Suora Teresa sent these for you.'

She looks up. 'Thank you! I will need them in an hour or two.'

'Has she always lived here?'

'During my lifetime. It was my favourite activity as a small girl, coming to visit her here at the Derelitti. All the nuns made a fuss of me. Among my parents' friends — there was a lot of silence when people saw my face. In those circles, a girl is only as worthwhile as her marriage prospects.'

I nod.

'From a young age, I knew this was where I would belong. People are kind. I have a purpose. The life of music, like the life of the mind, is the most valuable life we can live. And it is a joy to live close to my favourite great aunt!'

She offers me a biscuit and I shake my head.

'Can I help you at all, with this?'

'No. It's best if I keep going. But if you are interested in becoming a copyist, let Maestra Francesca know.'

As I walk back up the staircase to the dormitory, I realise I have never before considered where the copies of our music come from. So many silent tasks are involved in the creation of rapturous sound.

———

On Thursday morning, I go to the music room in preparation for Tonina's lesson. I am carrying Ombra, the cat, in my arms. He tries to clamber free, distracted by the smell of dried fish in my pockets. The fish oil will be difficult to remove from my clothes. It seems I will always have the remnants of fish on my person. I think back to Papà and the baskets of fish he would bring home.

In the music room, Ombra is more relaxed. He walks to each corner to sniff. Sometimes he puts out a paw as though to bat an invisible mouse. He pauses, sniffing the air. A shiver ripples through his fur. Then he comes closer and lifts himself to bump his head against my hand.

The tap comes at the door; I call out, but again I cannot be heard from this cell. Ombra steps back to investigate the spinet as I open the door. Tonina barely looks up as she comes inside. Then she sees the cat. She squeals with delight and drops her violin case to the floor with a thump. I watch as she runs towards the cat. He stands still, flicking his tail at the sudden movement. Tonina crouches down and rubs his head.

'Have you met Ombra, Tonina?' I ask.

She says nothing but a smile begins at the corners of her lips. I sit down with Tonina. The cat has rolled over now, revealing his soft belly, allowing Tonina to stroke him. When he tires of this and sits up, flicking his tail, I hand her some dried fish. She holds out a hardened morsel, and the cat clasps her hand with retracted claws. When she has fed him the first few pieces, I say to her, 'Now, Tonina. We are going to play the Tessarini slowly and work on the intonation. Then you can play with Ombra once more.'

She looks me full in the eye. She nods and takes up her violin.

# 9

On Friday morning, I splash cold water on my cheeks from the ceramic basin. I rub the liquid into the skin, pushing the crumbs of sleep out of my eyes. I dry my face with a small cloth. In the quiet, I tidy my hair, pulling the comb through to the rough ends. And then I cover it with my wimple.

Regina stands by the door, ready to come with me to matins.

'The *priora* has summoned me downstairs,' I tell her.

'Why?'

I shrug.

'See you at mass,' she says.

I walk quickly through the corridor to the foyer.

On the other side of the grille, Don Leonardi, is already pacing the floor in his green cloak. The cloak billows as he turns toward me. His leather shoes click on the tiles.

'I am sorry I kept you waiting,' I say.

'It was nothing.'

'I do not want to keep you from your work.'

He steps a little closer and smiles. 'You are not keeping me from work. Merely from my father, who wants me to speak with some of his clients.'

'What is the business?'

'We are merchants. It is all about trade. Cloth mainly.'

I nod.

'You did not bring your violin?'

'Was I supposed to?'

'I was hoping you would play for me again.'

I feel myself blushing to the covered-up roots of my hair.

'It is wondrous. I hope to hear you play a lot more.'

I stare down at the floor. I can hear the *priora*'s pen scratching across parchment at her small table on the other side of the grille. Is she listening to every word? Is she writing it down? I cannot think what to say.

'I went to the casino some days ago with my friends,' Don Leonardi says. I lift my eyes to his dark hair. 'It was marvellous! Many travellers were there. Men from England and France. They are not so quick with their cards as we Venetians!'

He smiles. 'You know, Lucietta — if I may call you that — you have beautiful hazel eyes. Quite an unusual colour.'

'Thank you.'

'May I come and see you again? I would very much like to know you better.'

'Of course.' Something is appealing about Don Leonardi and his tales of elsewhere. After he leaves, there is a lightness to my tread, my pulse fluttering quickly like the wings of a bird. When I return my thoughts to music, I realise that my mind has travelled far. For the time that we spoke, it was as though music had ceased to exist.

# 10

'Lucietta!' Mamma is reaching for my hand through the grille and I am shocked at the stinging in the corners of my eyes. While the bars might protect me from the outside world, at this moment, they have locked me in. I stare down for a moment, concentrating on the black and white tiles.

'What's wrong with her?' Papà asks.

I stare back at their faces. It is one month since I saw them. It is somehow both as though years have passed, and also as though I saw them yesterday. Mamma's skin is doughy, wisps of tangled grey escaping the threadbare bonnet around her ears. She looks old. She seems shorter and wider. Her brown

CHRISTINE BALINT

coat is lopsidedly pulled around her body. It has a
large stain like a damp patch on her breast. She is so
out of place here.

'Lucietta! You are so thin! Are they feeding you?'

'Of course,' my voice is strangely loud.

'Where is your beautiful hair? Why is it covered
up?'

'They cut it off.'

Tears spring to her eyes. She holds her hands to
her face. I look away.

'Pietro. They have cut off her hair.'

I reach under the wimple and feel my hair. It has
grown since it was cut. The ends are softer.

'I know. It will grow back.'

'But she is skinny and bald. Our beautiful girl . . .'

I rub my arms. Am I so ugly now? I reach over to
the chair and fall into it. I look through the grille to
where Maestra Francesca is sitting with the ledger
before her. She is staring at Mamma and Pietro.
Perhaps she has never before encountered a fisherman or a wet nurse. I shrink into my chair. For the
first time, I realise, I cannot go home. I will never
live with Mamma and Pietro again. I have begun
my life's work. I no longer belong in the domestic
sphere. Now that they have shorn my hair and a
nun's habit drapes my bony frame, I am not the girl
Mamma raised.

I swallow the wave of emotion that threatens to

erupt. I long to return to my music. But I must give Mamma and Pietro this time. For the time they gave me. I pluck at a loose thread above my knees.

In the silence, I hear a voice echo somewhere in the building. Something metal clattering to the floor. A soprano singing scales. In my mind, a sonata begins to play. The fingers of my right hand stiffen into a bow hold. My left-hand fingers curve around the strings in my mind to form notes.

'Lucietta!'

I jump at the sound of Pietro's voice.

'Are you meeting anyone?'

'The girls are quite friendly.'

'Just girls?'

Mamma looks up with her bloodshot eyes. I hesitate. Once, I would have them about Don Leonardi. I would have told them everything. But now, I am frightened of their coercion towards the life they have always imagined for me. In her mind, the music was a step towards a palazzo. If I moved from one domestic sphere to another, more elaborate one, she would still understand my life. The Derelitti would serve a function that could easily be discarded. But I have just begun my new life. I need to feel my way around it. I need to reach out and touch its boundaries and see if they are wide enough.

'Just girls.'

'No boys would be drawn to her now, Pietro.

Look at her. You can't even tell she's a girl.'

The words are as sharp as broken glass. I understand, now, that I can never return to her, nor can I ever be the person I used to be. I stand abruptly, trembling.

'I must go.'

Papà reaches his hand through the bars. His hands are cold, the skin rough. He has deep grooves in his forehead and around his eyes. He stands with his feet wide apart as though to balance. He smells of raw fish.

'It must be . .. . wonderful to work with other musicians. To find girls with the same interests as you.'

I swallow the sob in my throat. My voice wavers. 'It is wonderful, Papà. I feel that I belong here.'

# 11

The following Wednesday evening, we gather in the refectory with metal bowls filled with pale fish in a milky sauce. The thick floury flavour makes me nauseous, and I force the lumps down my throat with wine. At the *coro* table, we are given more nourishment, and our wine has less water; the sourness is hot in my stomach.

At the front of the room, Giuliana the violoncellist reads aloud from the book of Luke.

*'The disciple is not above his master: but every one that is perfect shall be as his master.'* As I chew my fish, I see that Regina has put down her fork and uses her good hand to twitch and twist and point at Agata sitting opposite. Agata is doing the same,

but she can keep eating with her right hand. And then Regina whispers that, after supper, we are to meet in the basement kitchen. I nod and pretend I have heard nothing. I pretend that I have no other thoughts or plans other than supper and compline.

I cannot eat the entire contents of my bowl. Regina is only halfway through hers when I look up, chasing the food around the sauce with a spoon. I put my hands in my lap; there is a new boniness to my frame — my ribs and hips are more clearly defined. I have hollows now. I do not go hungry, but I find myself eating only what I need. There is no pleasure in the food.

Regina looks at me from the corner of her eye, takes a final mouthful of sauce, and clatters the spoon in the dish. She stands from the table; Agata and I do the same. We usually leave our bowls in a basin to be taken down to the kitchen for washing, but tonight we take them down ourselves. Regina slips quickly down the stairs while Agata and I follow close behind.

Suora Teresa is wiping flour from a large table. She jumps when she sees us.

'We are just going to the coolroom; you did not see us,' Agata stacks our bowls by a basin next to two large cauldrons with lumpy white fluid caking the sides. It smells of old boiled fish. I bite my lip and lift my hand to my nose.

Suora Teresa laughs and shakes her head. Carrying a flickering lamp, Agata leads us to a small coolroom with shelves covered in bowls of fruit, plates of cheese and colourful jars of marinated vegetables. There are a basket of mussels and some marinated artichokes in a pale ceramic dish. There are sardines with finely sliced pickled onions. For a moment, I see Mamma holding out a plate of my favourite delicacy. Whenever Papà caught sardines, she kept them for me, asking Lionello to slice off their heads so that we would not have to see them looking at us as they marinated in vinegar and onion. Mamma was superstitious about the eyes of dead fish. She said they were the eyes of drowned sailors. I could not resist the flavour, and — even now — after supper, the aroma makes my mouth water.

Agata looks at me and laughs. She spoons the fragrant mixture into a smaller bowl and hands it to me. We could be three friends from the laneways in someone's mother's kitchen; we could be cousins.

'Suora Teresa does not see anything I do. Especially if it concerns the supplies.'

I pull my robe tighter around my body as I pick up flakes of the delicacy with a fork.

'What happened,' Regina says, 'What happened when Don Leonardi came back?'

I munch my fish. I imagine myself with these

girls in the years to come. Meeting in someone's kitchen in the future. Warmth and light and
laughter.

'He said he wanted to hear me play again.'

'Play what?'

'The violin, obviously.'

'Did he say where he wanted you to play? In his
house, perhaps? How long until you marry him?'

'Marry him?'

'Isn't that why you came here, to find a husband?'

'I– I came here to finish my training. He's not so
interesting.'

'Interesting? Isn't he Golden Book?' Regina's eyes
grow wide. 'You're not going to reject him?'

'Regina!' Agata says. 'Lucietta can make her own
decision.'

Regina glares at her.

I open my mouth and close it again. I look at
Regina as others must see her, as I saw her first — as
a girl with only one arm and few prospects.

I put down the bowl on the table and swallow. I
clasp my hands in front of me.

'I think that I am,' I whisper.

Regina gulps down a sob. 'But think of the life!
Think of the life you would have!'

The cry escapes her now, and she runs from the
room, leaving the door swinging behind her. In a
second, she is gone.

My breath is loud in my ears. Agata puts a hand on my wrist. 'When she was a child, her father told her she would be unmarriageable. Because of her missing arm. He sent her here so he could save his money for dowries for her sisters.'

So many things are required of me in this house of women. Until now, I was just a kind of daughter and sister and a studious, hard-working girl. Now I must learn how to perform friendship. 'Do they ever visit her?'

She shakes her head and takes our bowls to wash them in the basin.

—

Regina does not wait for me the following morning, and I make my way alone to vespers. The early morning light is glowing through the church windows as Maestra Francesca lifts her bow and the instruments trill like birds.

The nuns' voices hum from the church below; behind me, I hear the sopranos, Regina's strong sweet voice floating in the very centre of the note. After mass, as we make our way towards the stairs from the church balcony, I try to catch her eye. She looks away, clutching her empty sleeve with her good hand.

At lunchtime, I sit beside her. She picks slowly at her food with a fork.

'Regina, I am sorry if I offended you. But this life, this life of music — I am not sure I want to leave it. I would not have met you if not for being here.'

I hear her swallow. She looks up for a moment and then back down at her bowl. She replaces the spoon in the dish, stands from the table. She deposits the bowl in the basin with the dirty dishes and leaves the refectory.

At supper, Regina is listlessly stirring the thin broth. It is a watery soup with flecks of green in it. She is like a small child playing in a puddle outside the market.

'What is wrong, Regina?' I whisper. She continues stirring the soup. It is choppy like the lagoon in high wind.

'The men, the sons of the nobles. They always try to take the new girls away.'

'What do you mean?'

'Before you came, I had two other friends. Musicians. They played solos in the *sala della musica* and were noticed. They are gone now. Married into noble families. Off to their better lives. The palazzi with the servants. Me, I am still here. I will always be unmarriageable.' She stands and glares at me, tugging her empty sleeve. 'I will never leave.'

—

On Friday, after rehearsal, Maestra Francesca asks Regina and me to stay behind. All around, girls are gathering up papers and putting instruments in cases.

The girls stand with their music cases, whisper, wait for each other. In small groups, they leave. I walk to the front of the room with Regina, who does not look at me. Maestra Francesca is flipping through pages of parchment at her desk. She looks up and smiles.

'We need some new music for Carnevale. The archives have been in a mess for some time. I am wondering if you girls would mind taking on the task of organising them? See here.'

The wall is lined with ornate cupboards, dark wooden doors bordered with carved swirls. She approaches the closest one and turns the key. Inside is an untidy pile of papers. She pulls it out, and a cloud of dust rises in the air. She turns her head away from us and sneezes.

'Over the years, we have had many girls composing music for us. There is music here for every season. We need each piece with its parts. We need to check the orchestration. We need to throw out anything unreadable. Most of all, I want you to find the gold here. I cannot write and arrange music for every season; there's too much to do. I want you to find music we can use. Beginning with Carnevale.'

We meet in the cool afternoon before vespers. Regina has brought a small plate with two slices of orange upon it. I bite into the flesh, and sweet juice runs down my hands. Regina laughs and pulls a clean handkerchief from her pocket. We begin at the top shelf. I lift a pile of parchment down. We sit at opposite ends of the desk, each with a stack of yellowing paper with fading hurried notes.

'Oooh, listen to this!' Regina begins to sing a haunting melody of the Miserere. I can almost hear the composer singing across time. I flip through her pile and locate all the parts: soprano, alto, tenor, bass.

'Were there boys here?' I ask.

'No. The musicians were all girls. Four parts of female voices. Here, you check the instrumental parts . . .' she pats the sheets nearby.

'Regina, who wrote this music? Where are their names?'

'Some of it was by the Maestri: Pampani, Traetta and Sacchini. But a good deal of it was written by the members of the *coro*. They were girls like us. Trained in music. Their names are forgotten.'

Unwanted, unmarriageable girls through centuries. Here in this vast echoing building. Creating sublime music, their souls lost to time. Their music remaining.

And I see my part in restoring the music, in

finding their voices, trying to uncover their stories. And that this is a kind of legacy. A type of work that might sustain a life, more than the light, airy rooms of a palazzo or fading housedresses drying over the smoke of a fire.

# 12

Before supper on Saturday evening, I am practising downstairs when the *priora* comes.

'Lucietta, my dear, there is someone to see you.' Her voice from the silence startles me. Her face is still. Worried.

'Come down to the foyer when you are ready.'

I wait for her to tell me more so I can prepare myself. Could it be Don Leonardi returned so soon? What is his purpose in coming? She gives a faint apologetic smile and turns away. Her footsteps echo along the corridor growing even quieter.

I place my violin in its case and close it. I set it in the corner. As I walk along the corridor towards the church, I know that I am walking towards my future. Something is about to change. Someone is going to alter my direction.

A bell chimes somewhere outside. I am not sure which church is marking time for me now. I step out of the shadows. There is a single lamp on a table on the far side of the grille where the *priora* sits. The floral grate casts beautiful shadows in the dim light. She dips her quill in dark ink and scrawls. She does not look up from her work.

'Lucietta.' A man speaks my name; I jump. Now I see him standing two feet back from the grille in a black cloak. Although it is not Carnevale, he wears a plain white mask over his face, a pointed beak for a nose; I cannot make out his face. Grey curls emerge around his ears. His legs are spindly; his voice has the tremor of age.

I cannot sit down. I am one foot from the ornate walls of my cage but fixed in place.

'We have not met before. I am your father.'

I am shaking now, rendered mute.

'I am pleased that you have proven yourself so teachable . . . I hear that you are an accomplished musician. You do understand — you understand that gives you an opportunity now, one not given to many raised in your circumstances.'

He has been observing my life from afar. Someone has been informing on me. Someone I trusted has revealed me to this stranger without revealing him to me. Who was it? And why is he here? Is it curiosity or fear that I will not follow his plan? Fear that I will refuse his demands? I wonder if he is a Pisani, a Loredan or a Mocenigo. I wonder which palazzo holds my relations and the ghosts of my ancestors. I wait for him to tell me his name.

'I hear you will soon have a suitable offer of marriage. You must take this offer. You will have a life that wants for nothing. You are free to leave your lowly beginnings behind. You will not have to struggle for your living or to work.'

Who has told him of my suitor? Has he been moving me through my life like a pawn on a chessboard? And after all my training, what could there possibly be in my life if not work? I have been preparing for it since childhood.

The man paces up and down on the other side of the grille as though it is he who is caged. I want to cover my ears. I want to hide beneath the floor, to sink into the lagoon and not hear another word. But he does not stop.

'This afternoon, I made my final payment on your behalf. It is the end of my responsibility. I hope you can see that I have more than fulfilled my obligations. This payment is your dowry. Once I have paid it, you must marry. You will be gone from this place.

To a better life that befits my daughter.'

I am sobbing now, keening in grief. The sound is uncontrollable. I hear the *priora* push her chair back and stride over.

'That is enough. You may leave. Just tell the child, tell Lucietta because I am sure she wants to know: who is her mother?'

He laughs then. 'Her mother? Her mother was a lowly woman who was in my employ. She . . . showed kindness to me. I had to let her go to protect my family's reputation. That was what my father said at the time. *Priora*, I will await your word that my instructions have been followed.'

'Tell me more.' My voice comes unbidden. 'Tell me about my mother.'

The man softens. He bows his head. His voice, when it comes, is a softer timbre. 'She had a beautiful singing voice. She had been trained at the Derelitti, I believe.' He reaches into his pocket and pulls out a crumpled piece of parchment that he gives to the *priora*.

'Who was she?' I whisper, but the words are drowned in tears. As I struggle to speak, I hear the door from the foyer opening. I hear the footsteps of fine-heeled shoes. The *priora* does not speak, but — beneath my keening — I hear the key turning in the lock of the grille. A moment later, the key turns again to lock me inside. My work with the world outside is done for now. I do not know when I will ever again set foot outside these walls.

There are light footsteps as she comes to me. And then I can feel her arms tightening around me, and all I can do is keep my eyes closed and weep.

—

When I am weak and trembling and empty, the *priora* sits back on her heels.

'Lucietta.'

Her face is wrinkled, eyes bloodshot, some white locks of hair are visible beneath the wimple. 'Your mother must have given him her half of this wind chart for you. They must have seen each other after you were gone.' The scrap is faded and torn; its surface creased. I can just make out the carefully ruled points showing the *ponente*, the direction of the sunset and the *tramontane*, the north wind, the direction of anything uncanny or foreign. In the corner, in fading ink, I make out the name Chiara de Basso.

'We do not need to make a decision now. But Lucietta, there is a home for you here. You can remain as a musician. You are free to remain here and have meaningful work for your lifetime. As you know, you are already earning income from your performances and teaching. And, if you feel called, you can think about becoming a nun.'

She takes my arm, and I force myself to stand.

And then I notice how small she is, how bird-like her frame. I know that God has led to me to this moment. He kept me safe. Gave me gifts and allowed me to be educated. But not for a moment have I felt called to anything other than music.

She leads me up the spiral staircase, away from the dormitory. There is cell after cell along a corridor, each door wooden and polished. She turns the key in a lock, pushes the door. There is a narrow bed along a wall. The other wall has a small table. A lamp. A quill and ink. A small window above.

'You may sleep here while we decide what is to be done.'

I see now that she is bent over, frail, more so than when I arrived. I have aged her. I have brought troubles to her house. How long has she known my father? How long has she known of her responsibility? What is her role in this story?

I think now of my birth mother, Chiara. She must have been young and beautiful — at the mercy of her master. It is a familiar story. From their first encounter, she would have been powerless. Men with money have driven this city and all the life I have known. The Golden Book and its gold. I am half Golden Book. It is a label I longed for as a small child. And now that I have seen it in the flesh, it is repugnant to me. Without it, I would not exist. And now, according to the orphanages' creed, my life's purpose is to help atone for the sins of the city through music.

Did he try to win her favour? Did she think she loved him? Where did she go when he banished her?

In my cell, I lose track of time. Suora Teresa brings me a plate of boiled eggs. Some watery wine. The dry eggs catch in my throat. The sour wine makes my head spin.

I watch the light bleed from the window. And then there is a knock at the door. Maestra Francesca enters with my violin. She sits on the chair.

'The *priora* said you were unwell.'

I do not know what to say. I do not lift my head from the pillow.

'Lucietta, I need you in the *coro*. The melody is too thin. Rest tonight. But if you are well enough, please come to matins.'

She sits quietly for a moment. Then I hear the chair scraping on the floor. The door clicks open and then closed.

And now I am alone in the cold dark silence. It is vast. In my mind, I see Mamma frying fish over the fire. She is joking with Pietro, a single hand on the skillet, laughing. And I wonder how much of my story she knew. I long for her with a deep ache.

I open my eyes in the darkness, and there is a sliver of moonlight on the wall. All my life, I thought Mamma wanted me to save my hands and my mind and my fingers for music out of love. Perhaps she had no choice.

I do not know what life with a nobleman would entail. I try to imagine a room full of windows and light. Looking out over the water at the gondolas passing by. But the space presents a different kind of confinement. And the isolation of it is frightening. I like Don Leonardi well enough, at a distance. But to submit to him is another thing. To be dependent on him for my understanding of my life. To have to learn under him the rules of the Golden Book. To rely on him for all my connections in the world. To have to surrender my purpose. A married woman does not work seriously as a musician. She may play occasionally for guests. But her primary purpose is to maintain the household and her husband's social standing. Have I devoted my life to music simply to exchange it for what others see as a better life? Am I to have no say at all in my future?

And Lionello. Lionello in his large clumsy frame, his workboots. His knowledge of how a harpsichord functions and his ignorance of the art found in a palazzo. How can I go forward in life without the hope of seeing him? If I were to marry a nobleman, I may never know Lionello's children. Or share with them the days of playing in the laneways, of watching my brother dive a neat arc into the lagoon.

I want to talk to someone, but there is only air

and moonlight. I wonder if I have been locked in. I stand up from the bed, sliding my feet towards the door. I run my fingers up the wood, and I'm relieved when I feel the iron key. It turns smoothly in the lock, and the door swings open. There are small windows in the corridor, and they allow moonlight to push through into the darkness. I have been housed with the nuns. I hear prayerful whispering from behind a door. I step back into my cell. Relock the door. Try to sleep.

—

In the morning, I wake with the angelus. I have slept in my robes, but I manage to smooth them with my hands. There is a small basin of cold water on the table. I splash my cheeks — the water tastes of salt. I pull a comb through the stiff tufts of hair. It feels dry, foreign. I take the wimple and pull it tight over my head. I feel the line of cloth around my hairline. I am fully covered.

In the church balcony, I take up my instrument. I close my eyes, tightening and adjusting my fingers to tune the strings. I stroke the violin. It is the one constant on my journey — wherever I go. Small groups of girls in robes arrive together, moving their hands in soft gestures I know are really words. They are speaking sotto voce. Never silent. They move slowly so they can appear pious, but they are communicating with gestures.

And then the slight figure of the *priora* is walking towards me, her white robes flowing around her legs. She reaches me and stops. She nods at me in greeting, peering at me all the while. I have tried to wash the tears from my skin. I have tried to smooth away the ache of yesterday, to push away the heaviness in my heart.

The *priora* sees the violin at my side. She smiles and bows her head at me. She places a hand on my arm; she is closer now, staring at my eyes. She steps back, removes her hand. I feel the warmth of it. Then she turns and continues walking.

In this place of silence, we seldom speak. Music is our voice. The weight of her hand, the warmth of it, the smile and the nod. This is all I have, but it is the world.

# Acknowledgements

*Water Music* is a work of imagination drawing on the unique history of the musical orphanages of Venice, in place from around 1400 to 1797. These early music conservatories were run for and by women. They enabled women to pursue professional careers when this was rarely possible elsewhere in the world; their music met the highest international performance standards. The unique system of patronage that gave talented orphan girls a full-time musical education came to an end with the Napoleonic invasion of Venice in 1797.

I would like to thank the Foundation for Literary Studies (FALS) at James Cook University and Brio Books for their generous sponsorship of Viva la Novella IX. This project was made possible by funding from Creative Victoria, The Australia Council and the

Marten Bequest Travelling Scholarship. In Venice, I was privileged to access the archives of Santa Maria dei Derelitti in the Istituzioni di Ricovero e di Educazione Venezia, under the directorship of Dr Giuseppe Ellero — at a time when it was possible to do so. I also studied the papers of the late musicologist Jane Baldauf-Berdes, now housed in the special collections room at Duke University Library, North Carolina. Baldauf-Berdes devoted her career to researching the musical orphanages of Venice. Her book, *Women Musicians of Venice* (Oxford University Press, 1993), remains a seminal text in this branch of musicology.

The Melbourne Women's Choir, directed by Faye Dumont, and Bel Canto women's choir, directed by Margaret Brown, provided me with opportunities to sing music written for the orphan girls of Venice. Enormous thanks to Faye Dumont for assisting me with early research and for later fact-checking. Any remaining errors are my own.

In 2016, I was fortunate to travel to Venice with the Melbourne Women's Choir to perform some of this repertoire in the Pietà church in Venice and other European cities. Thank you to Faye Dumont, Ann Roberts and Lynda Campbell, who gave precious time in Venice to helping me uncover and explore the locations for this novella.

I am very grateful to my writing colleagues, Wendy Orr and Steven Conte, who generously read previous versions of this work. Dr Antoni Jach and fellow masterclass workshoppers also provided insightful feedback and support.

I would like to thank Michelle and David May for their friendship and for providing me with a church studio in which to work.

I am grateful to Lia Passadori for assisting with primary source documents.

Thank you to my husband, Rupert, who read many drafts and shared research journeys both as a researcher and to look after our children. I am grateful to my parents-in-law, Angela and Tim Smith, who travelled to Venice with us to look after my young daughter. Thank you to Imogen and Raphael for their patience.

Sadly, in the years since I began writing, fire has damaged a section of the church of the Derelitti — including the ceiling fresco. It is still possible to visit the church; however, it is no longer in regular use. The distinctive *sala della musica* has fortunately been preserved.

This project was supported by the Victorian Government through Creative Victoria.

This project has been assisted by the Australian Government through the Australia Council, its arts funding and advisory body.

# VIVA
## LA NOVELLA

Viva la Novella is an annual prize awarded for short works between twenty and fifty thousand words. Since its beginnings in 2013 the award has published sixteen short novels by sixteen outstanding authors.

For more information, please visit our website
www.seizureonline.com

### VIVA LA NOVELLA 2021 WINNERS
*Water Music* by Christine Balint
9781922267610 (print) | 9781922598363 (digital)

*Every Day is Gertie Day* by Helen Meany
9781922267627 (print) | 9781922598370 (digital)

### VIVA LA NOVELLA 2020 WINNERS
*Late Sonata* by Bryan Walpert
9781922267238 (print) | 9781922267245 (digital)

*Dark Wave* by Lana Guineay
9781922267252 (print) | 9781922267269 (digital)

### VIVA LA NOVELLA 2019 WINNERS
*Listurbia* by Carly Cappielli
9781925589870 (print) | 9781925589887 (digital)

*Offshore* by Joshua Mostafa
9781925589894 (print) | 9781925589900 (digital)

### VIVA LA NOVELLA 2018 WINNERS
*Swim* by Avi DuckorJones
9781925589504 (print) | 9781925589511 (digital)

*The BedMaking Competition* by Anna Jackson
9781925589528 (print) | 9781925589535 (digital)